HEIDEGGER STAIRWELL

A NOVEL

WINNER OF THE 34TH ANNUAL INTERNATIONAL 3-DAY NOVEL CONTEST

HEIDEGGER STAIRWELL

A NOVEL

BY KAYT BURGESS

3-DAY BOOKS

VANCOUVER • TORONTO

Heidegger Stairwell
Copyright © 2012 by Kayt Burgess

All rights reserved. No part of this book may be reproduced by any means without the prior permission of the publisher, with the exception of brief passages in reviews.

This is a work of fiction. Any resemblance to persons either living or deceased is purely coincidental.

Book design and cover photography by Mauve Pagé
Edited by Kris Rothstein

Distributed in Canada by University of Toronto Press and in the United States by Consortium through Arsenal Pulp Press (www.arsenalpulp.com).

PUBLISHED BY
3-Day Books
PO Box 2106, Station Terminal
Vancouver, BC V6B 3T5
Canada

info@3daynovel.com
www.3daynovel.com

Printed in Canada

LIBRARY AND ARCHIVES CANADA CATALOGUING IN PUBLICATION

Burgess, Kayt, 1981–
  Heidegger Stairwell / Kayt Burgess.

Issued also in electronic format.
ISBN 978-1-55152-486-3

  I. Title.

PS8603.U7366H45 2012   C813'.6
C2012-901139-8

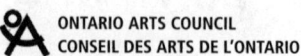 ONTARIO ARTS COUNCIL
CONSEIL DES ARTS DE L'ONTARIO

We thank the Ontario Arts Council for their support of this project.

The interior of this book is printed on Rolland Enviro 100, containing 100% post-consumer recycled fibers, Eco-Logo certified, processed without chlorinate, FSC® Recycled and manufactured using biogaz energy.

To my Family
And to all the musicians
with whom I've collaborated
over the years.

Editor:

Sorry for being out of touch these last weeks. I was in Mexico and then... I trust you heard what happened. In that light, some of this is in poor taste but I haven't touched anything with that new filter.

This manuscript got away on me. I'm terrified of what the band's going to say. They're petty bastards. If any of them have notes, please compile and **edit** them for my sake.

—Evan Strocker

Freeman Shuffle
BERLIN, NOVEMBER 2011

Six-thirty-five on Saturday night, I'm riding the elevator to the penthouse with a soft-faced, straw-haired German bellhop in a navy blue uniform. He looks like the Cabbage Patch doll I decapitated when I was six. I ask him if this is the hotel where Hitler stayed and Göring got married, or if it's the hotel where Hitler stayed and Michael Jackson dangled his son off the balcony. The bellhop, in perfect English, tells me he doesn't speak English.

The elevator's skeleton is gilded, the glass and mirror smudged with fingerprints. "Marcus" has written his name on the window with his oily finger, as has "Scheiße." The bellhop notices and buffs out the graffiti with his sleeve. He apologizes, as though it is a personal attack against me and a great humiliation for his people. His apology is also in perfect English.

I get off at the top floor. The band has the run of the entire level, and there's some guy standing at the entrance. He pats me down. He asks me why I have two cell phones. I tell him one's a radio detonator. He asks me again. I give him the same answer but tell him the bomb is in Prague. And it's fake. He finds the 9mm in my suit jacket and asks me why I have it. I tell him it's to protect my fake bomb and show him the empty barrel. I assure him my Gucci shoes are real, but I'm lying. I make a joke about *mein Pimmel* which he wouldn't get because he didn't strip search me, unlike the goons at LAX, or half the airports I've been to over the last few years. Then again, I did recently write an exposé on how easy it is to smuggle amphetamines through customs, so I suppose that's my fault.

He asks if my name is Evan Strocker. I tell him it is, legally, even. He confiscates my phones and my gun and directs me down the hall to the suite.

The hallway walls are wood-panelled—not that seventies shit my parents had in the nineties, but the classy European kind. Label people, or random entourage people, pass by. One fat guy in jeans and aviator reading glasses stops me, tells everyone it's been ages since we've seen each other, and congratulates me on the airport piece. I was a fucking hero, and did I bring the band anything, wink wink. No, but thanks, I say, pat his shoulder and call him bud because I can't remember his name. Actually, I don't think I know the guy.

One of the band's two bodyguards is stationed outside the suite. I can hear yelling from behind the double doors. The bodyguard says hey to me in English, which means the French one's inside. The fight starts to break up and I hear the baby crying. The bodyguard tells me I can go inside just as I'm closing the door behind me.

Ceramic shards crunch underfoot as I enter the foyer. Broken mug. Everything smells of the coffee splashed on the wall, thick and dark and speckled with grinds. I find my way to the living room (drawing room? parlour?). It's like the background in a baroque portrait, all velvet drapes, paisley sofas and a flame in the fireplace. There's a faint, grandmotherish smell of Earl Grey, date squares and mentho-lyptus. It's a long way from prefab bungalows with blankets covering the windows to keep out the Northern Ontario draft. But the company's not so different.

On the sofa, bright blue Converse propped up on the arm, knee popping through a hole in his jeans, soft, hairy abdomen drooping out from under the hem of his rugby shirt, eyes closed, mouth open, drool pooling on the throw pillow and collecting in his beard, sleeps my old friend William Sacco, sound despite recent chaos. The band has a photo album full of candid shots of

Will falling asleep at unfortunate times, in the most compromising positions, all over the world. Fans know this because of the sophomore album song "Will Sleeps It Off." But some photo highlights that didn't make the song include Will Sleeps It Off Whitewater Rafting, Will Sleeps It Off at the Junos, Will Sleeps It Off in a Sweaty Hooker's Lap, Will Sleeps It Off in the Heritage Minister's Lap and Will Sleeps It Off Sitting on a Port Authority Shitpot.

I kick Will like I used to when we were kids, in the leg, which sometimes woke him up with a charley horse. He calls me a MacQueen faggot before rolling over on his side.

"In Will's defence, there are three MacQueens staying here, so statistically..."

The voice casts a long shadow bisecting the living room (drawing room? parlour?). I doubt anyone who's ever heard that voice can forget it: full-bodied and resonant, complex, a little creamy, although it's sounding raspy these days, which explains the smell of menthol. Three months touring, singing five arenas a week will do it.

Torq MacQueen leans against the doorframe, all smiles despite the blood-shot eyes. The baby's still crying in the background. The French bodyguard is still hanging out in the hallway near what looks to be a study or office. I can guess who's in there.

"You look like shit," I say. Shit's a relative term, though.

He scratches at his stubble. "Yeah." He still has an hour to hit the phone booth and turn into a rock star.

That rock star pulls me out my chair and gives me a good thump on the back. He smells one part grandma, one part baby food and one part gym equipment. Torq fingers my jacket and pulls away, subtly sniffing at his spit-up-encrusted sweater. He pulls it off and drops it on Will, whom he kicks as he passes. Will swats at him, semiconscious.

"Want a drink?" Now in his threadbare Joy Division t-shirt and sagging jeans, Torq goes to the bar and opens one of the panels, pulling out a bottle of some green potion. He sees my face and rolls his eyes, grabbing two glasses from the open shelf behind the bar. Torq pours my whisky with a splash of water; he takes his vegan smoothie neat. Handing me the glass, he collapses in the chair by the fire, deflated, running a hand through that shaggy dark emo hair he's not allowed to change.

I raise my glass to him. "To notorious trendster womanizers neutered by domesticity."

He lifts his eyebrow and his glass. "To smug douchebags who are still alive despite all odds."

We drink.

Smooth. Mental note to take the bottle with me.

"I was surprised you called," says Torq. Have to hand it to him to drink that without even a grimace. "I thought you were in London doing a story on blue-eyed soul. Then I hear you're on the Continent, bombing Prague even."

"Music's my first love, but I get tired of listening to other people yammer about themselves. Especially musicians."

"But listening to *you* talk about yourself is completely different..."

I ignore him. "Sometimes you need to just *do* something. It's an itch."

Torq nods thoughtfully. "My daughter gets that. Coco puts powder on it and the kid doesn't blow up Prague."

"She's fifteen months. Give her twice as many years and we'll see." The baby's still crying. I can't tell where it's coming from because it seems to be everywhere all at once. She inherited some good pipes, I'll give her that. "What's she on about?"

"Hell if I know." He puts up his empty glass. "What're you doing here, Ev?"

"I'll tell you mine if you tell me what you and Pierre were French-fighting about."

He props his combat boots on the coffee table. "That obvious?"

"If you were fighting with your babymama the French bodyguard would've been outside the door."

He snorts. "Other people in the band fight besides me. Will's the most belligerent bastard I've ever met. Fuckhead's sleeping off a brawl with a German cowboy. Who knew they had cowboys in Deutschland?"

HEIDEGGER STAIRWELL 11

Sure, people fight. Musicians always squabble. But no one fights like Torq because no one cares as hard as he does. "What're you fighting about?"

"Nothing. Strings for a new song. Tune's only half written and Pierre's already pushing these Paderewski-style horror show violin backings. They're cool enough when your ears aren't haemorrhaging, but our audience won't get it. He's being deliberately abstruse to piss me off. Baby woke up and Coco lost it on us, but mostly me because I am apparently chronically useless as a father and a partner and a singer."

I don't really want to talk about his domestic problems, but I'd be remiss if I didn't at least ask. "So you and Coco are . . . good?"

"We're on tour." He says that like it's an answer. "I can't believe how young you still look. We're the same age but I feel like I'm a hundred years old."

"Don't worry about it—sixteen-year-olds are still making fan sites about your cheekbones. And not just the slutty ones who lost their virginity when they were ten and have moved on to sixty-year-old cock."

His look is blasé.

"It's the hormones," I remind him. "And I don't have a human air-raid siren keeping me up all night."

Just to spite my point, the baby stops crying. Torq closes his eyes, breathes a sigh of relief. Down the hall, someone closes a door—just the faint click of the latch bolting. Torq slinks as low into the chair as possible, as though he's going to drip right off the seat. I consider calling the English-speaking bodyguard.

Coco Coburn stands in the doorframe, her strawberry blond hair a nest around her head, crusted with baby barf, bangs shiny with oil and sweat. Last night's eye makeup is melting down her cheeks and her puffy-lipped mouth dry, cracked, frowning. She's wearing Torq's Wham! t-shirt and it's smeared with something green that looks vaguely like Torq's cocktail, but definitely doesn't smell like it. No wonder Torq has his eyes closed—his brain's exploding trying to reconcile memories of his glamorous partner with . . . well, with this.

"Are you stupid?" That's directed at Torq. Coco hasn't even noticed me.

Somehow he manages to slither even lower in the chair. "Yes. Yes I am."

Coco rubs her forehead with the back of her hand. "Goddamn it, I just got her down. An hour to myself—is that really too much to ask for? And then you..." She grits her teeth and fans her eyes. In vain—a big fat tear slides down her greasy cheek. "When she cries she shits. She shits all over!" Now Coco's bawling, rubbing her eyes with her shit-stained palm, snivelling between trembling inhalations. "I hate you; I hate everyone in this band. I'm so tired. I just want to go to my own bed."

Torq stands and wraps his arms around her. He flinches and breathes through his mouth. "Me too."

"I don't care what you want," she growls. "You're a lazy asshole. And you sneak in my bed again and I'm going to castrate you, donate your dick to Evan."

"It doesn't work that way," I say, casual. "But thank you in advance for thinking about me when you mutilate your man, Coco."

She sees me and smiles, beatific. "Hi Evan. It's nice to see you. You look really handsome in your suit. I'd give you a hug but..."

"—you're covered in shit, I heard." Problem solver that I am, I hug her from behind. I did not know women could smell this bad. I count to three and let go.

Torq kisses her forehead. "We have an hour till we head out for the stadium. Go have a bath, relax." He takes the baby monitor necklace off her neck, puts it around his own.

"Really?" She sounds so relieved. Watching all this makes me thankful I'll never father a child.

"I'll join you in a bit," says Torq. "I'll get my brother to listen for her if he's not stoned."

"He's stoned. Ask Isis," says Coco. "Wait—we broke up yesterday. Get off me." She brushes him off. "Nice to see you Evan." I try not to squirm when she kisses my cheek, or when she whispers, "If you write about this, be gentle with me, 'kay?" She wanders down the hall, sliding her hand along the walls to keep herself standing.

For the record, the above descriptions are gentle.

Torq collapses in his chair, toying with the monitor. A heavenly static crackles.

"Broke up, huh?"

He rolls his eyes.

"Is Coco gonna be okay to sing tonight?" I ask.

"She's hardcore."

"I think she's having a nervous breakdown."

"Yeah, well." Torq pretends to hang himself with the baby monitor.

It feels like old times, but I'm stalling. I don't really know how to broach the topic, so I'll just come out with it. "So I'm writing a memoir."

"Yeah."

"Coco told you," I accuse.

"You know better. Plus, it was her idea, wasn't it?"

I nod.

"If she didn't tell anyone she couldn't take credit."

"What else did she tell you?"

Torq shrugs. "That she convinced you to write a memoir. Tony got you a publisher for it. I don't know why anyone would want to read a book about you, but people seem to read your 'articles' so what do I know?"

Coco has strategically left out the most important part. "It's not just about me, Torq. The book's about you guys—about growing up with you. A backstage pass to Heidegger Stairwell's origin story."

He mulls that over, his silver-screen face manifesting every flick of emotion. "So, a compilation of all the articles you've written about us over the last decade?"

"No. More like an in-depth look at everything I haven't written about."

Torq blinks. A curious smile plays on his lips. "Are you selling us out?"

"It was Coco's idea," I remind him, quickly.

He shrugs, laughing. "I'm not angry. It's fine. We write about you—you know you have carte blanche to write about us. But..."

Ellipses make me nervous. "What?"

"You've never asked permission before. So why now? And why're you asking *me*?"

I stand. "It doesn't matter. You're right. Carte blanche. Thanks."

Often I recreate Torq MacQueen in my mind as vapid because he's a handsome rockstar, but truth is he's much smarter than I am, as he proves by saying, "I'm a dry run."

I deny it, but he doesn't buy it.

"What're you afraid he's going to say?" says Torq.

"I'm afraid he's going to say nothing."

Torq considers that. "That's probably what he'll say."

"So then I should just not tell him."

Torq's not fooled. "Why'd you come here then, Evan?"

Torquil MacQueen is insufferable company, which is why I leave him in the living room (drawing room? parlour?) and not because he's right and I have no retort.

I pass the study. The door's ajar and through the crack I spy a vertical slice of Pierre Clowes working, tireless and manic, at a grand walnut desk covered in manuscript paper. His grey-streaked hair is shaggy, his long face splotched red, eyes round and bugged. Even locked in a frenetic ideas dump, he is wearing his trademark tweed jacket and kelly-green tie. Pierre catches me watching him. Glare. Door slam.

I've never been his favourite person. I suppose I can't fault him for that, considering I'm an asshole, but he doesn't have to be so French expressing it. All that anger's going to give him a heart attack.

Next in this never-ending suite is the media room, where Isis Wong sits by herself watching German infomercials. She is clean, her hair is brushed, I can't smell her from across the room, and she's dressed for the stage in a silky slate-grey short jumpsuit, high-heeled combat boots and a bone and shell necklace she wears like a breastplate. Her unnatural platinum blond hair is shaggy, asymmetrical, as perfectly unkempt as their stylist can sculpt, and her makeup is ethereal.

Without tearing her eyes from the television she says, "Next time you bolt, leave the remote."

"You could get up and change the channel, like we did in the old country."

Isis looks up, her mouth opening in a perfect O. "Evan."

"Hey, you got my name right," I tease.

"It's only been three years," she says. She doesn't remember what she called me the last time we saw each other. Or she's refusing to play along. She was never one to indulge me and there has always been something about her rhythm that throws me off. She's a terrible straight man and not just because she happens to be a lesbian. Isis would say good friends aren't there to feed your bad jokes. I'm not sure what sort of friends we are anymore, though.

"What are you doing here?" she asks

Jack LaLanne is selling juicers on the flat screen in German. I manually mute the television. "I'm writing a memoir."

"I know. Coco told me."

No one's ever accused Coco of keeping a secret too well. "Okay."

"Have you started it?"

I stall. "Almost done, actually."

"Does it paint us all as stupid, self-absorbed assholes with arrested development and personality disorders?"

I'm hurt. "Why would you think that?"

"Because it's true. Every day I have to stop myself from pushing one of these people out a window." She sits back on her sofa, one leg tucked under her, resuming her state of readiness. "Lugh's in the next suite. I'm assuming you're looking for him. Good luck with that. When you see him, tell him to bring back the remote."

Lugh MacQueen is on the balcony, bent over his guitar. He's tucked himself into the corner by the railing, taking up as little space as possible. The balcony rail is white-washed wrought iron and through the banisters Berlin presents its wonders: manicured parks, restored red brick, dramatically lit fountains, and a cluster of paparazzi snapping photos of Heidegger Stairwell's lead guitarist sitting above them, outside in November, shirtless, wearing a bushman's beard, smoking a blunt, on the balcony where MJ may or may not have dangled his son. I'm going to have to chase down those vultures so I can get art for the book.

The sweet smell of hashish and the sound of suspended chords fill the air. He's added a new tattoo since I last saw him: the neck of a guitar running the length of his spinal cord, leading into a photoreal tuning head inked on the nape of his neck. There's a fret for every vertebra, and seven strings like on his Ibanez. As he fingerpicks his acoustic, I can almost see black dots appear and disappear on the fretboard along his spine, as though his back were a series of chord charts. My perfect ear, inherited from my mother, has always been the key to translating Lugh MacQueen's moods, as much as anyone can.

Critics and media bloggers have accused Lugh of contriving his mystery, but they're just jaded. The enigma of Lugh MacQueen is authentic and infuriating. It's been years since I've had an encounter with him that didn't end with me wanting to punch him in his glass eye.

"Isis wants the remote back."

He switches to a C-sharp suspended four. Neither major nor minor. Torq always gets well-structured chords from Lugh—I get wasteland harmonies.

As quick as his hands move along the neck of the guitar, his body moves sloth-like, the weed at work. He leans the guitar against the rail, stands, and pulls the remote from the pocket of his jeans. Lugh doesn't look at me when he offers it, or when I take it. All I have is a good look of the pubic-like dark hair hanging from his jaw and the rottweiler tattoo on his bicep. Without a word, he's back on his stool with his guitar playing progressions of suspended chords with the occasional blues base line woven through. I didn't expect anything more.

"I'm writing a book," I say to the guitar on his back. "Tony got this publishing deal for me. It's like a bio-memoir thing."

He stops playing, letting the last plucked string ring. "About you?" he says in that smoke-and-shambles voice he uses to back his brother.

"That's kinda what a memoir is." I try to inject some levity in the exchange, but he goes back to his guitar. "But it's about Heidegger too."

A minor chord out of place in the progression. "Are you looking for my blessing?"

"I just wanted to tell you."

He resolves the minor chord. "I'm happy for you, Ev."

I can't tell if he's being obtuse or avoidant, so I just lay the cards out. "I'll be writing about you."

A diminished seventh. "I know."

"Not about your music. About you."

"Do whatever you want. You always do."

I get the message without him having to play an obnoxious dissonance. He's more subtle than that anyway—he plays an old blues lick. He wants me gone. I don't blame him. The last time I saw him I broke old Ibanez's neck. Seeing it on his back, I remember how that guitar felt in my hand, hot from overuse, the wood saturated with inexpressible emotion from a lifetime with one-eyed Lugh. The band's manager, Tony, is still forwarding me hate mail from fans who want my blood for killing that guitar. I don't regret it, but I regret everything else I said and did that day.

I turn to the sliding glass door. "Thanks for the remote. I'll give it to Isis on my way out."

Nothing but suspension.

"I'll see you around, Lugh MacQueen."

Lugh slips into finger picking, ambiguous fifths and minor ninths, and sings:

> *"There once was a girl named Evie*
> *Full of laughter, full of lies*
> *Every trick was her taking cover*
> *Every joke, a worn disguise*

> *She left me a pile of rosewood*
> *She left her a string of goodbyes*
> *And Evie, the girl for me*
>
> She died."

I want to punch his good eye, now. But I'm shaking with sadness and rage and I'm afraid he'll duck and I'll look like an asshole in front of the paparazzi. "Evie was a crazy bitch," I say.

He stops playing. From inside, there's yelling, screaming, swearing, male and female, in both official languages of our placid homeland. Lugh stabs his blunt into the rail, grabs his guitar and follows the ruckus. I trail.

In the hallway by the washroom, underneath an ornately framed Dutch etching, on the marble floor, Isis Wong is in the process of breaking up a fistfight between Torq and Pierre. Torq is straddling Pierre—flailing, throwing wild punches, yelling in French—while trying to keep Isis out of the way. Lugh jumps in, tackles his brother, pinning Torq's arms behind his back. Pierre lunges after the MacQueens but Isis grabs him, holds him down. Surprised, he tries to rip himself away and elbows her in the face. Isis falls hard on her back, winded, eyes wide, mouth gulping, face darkening to purple.

It shuts them up. The hall is silent until Isis takes her first breath. From the bathroom, we can hear Coco singing a passage from *Lucia di Lammermoor*, none the wiser behind her earphones.

Will stumbles out of the living room pulling up his jeans, squinting at the light. "What the fuck is . . . 'Sup Evan?"

I help Isis up. She slaps me away. She's trembling.

"The hell's with the lesbot?" Will looks down at the MacQueens. Lugh still hasn't given Torq back his limbs. "Which one of you assholes kept kicking me? And why're you cuddling? You know normal guys don't do that shit."

"I'm so done," says Isis. She spits into her hand, her phlegm bloody. "I'm going to play this gig and then I'm taking the first flight back to Toronto."

Torq finally kicks his brother off and stands. "You can't do that. We still have another three weeks on the Continent and two shows in Britain."

"Torquil MacQueen, you're not my jailer, you're just a singer. A singer who can't even hit the notes he's paid for anymore."

"This isn't about me, Isis."

"Everything is always about you," she snaps, advancing on Torq. "It's about you being such a camera skank that we have no privacy and have to be smuggled into hotels on lockdown because someone is inevitably going to try to kill you again."

"Isis, that's not cool," I say.

"And you're so fucking lazy, Torq—you wanted that baby so badly and yet you never do anything to help Coco with that goddamn puking, screaming, shitting nightmare that is turning your wife into a psycho. In fact, you make her life harder by being such a tyrant about these new songs. FYI, I hate these songs, they're derivative and pop and cater to the lowest common denominator, so you better unzip your pants for the cover because you're whoring us out again."

Pierre parrots the sentiment in his accented English, which is the stupidest thing to do because Isis turns on him. "And you. What the hell are you doing here? Lurking?" Her voice falls to a quiet seethe. "Get cozy with your hand and stop taking out your sexual frustration on everyone. These orchestrations are weird and creepy. It makes me miss the days you were coked out of your mind."

Lugh slips out of the hall, back to his balcony. But Isis doesn't miss it. "Big surprise—One-Eyed Lugh walks away. Any conflict at all, just fucking walks out the door." She has to stop to take a breath.

Will, in typical fashion, is prepping for his turn. He looks like he's going to start a Maori haka. Isis just rolls her eyes. "I'm not going to waste my breath on you. Why don't you go sleep this off?" She turns away from him and passes by me, taking the remote.

"Isis. Are you quitting?" I ask.

She lingers. "I don't know, *Evan*. May I? Will you allow it? I love how we have to stay the same, together, forever, but you can just up and leave whenever you want. Change your style, change your name, change your goddamn sex." She motions at Torq, Will, Pierre. "Get to it, Evan—try to fix us. Why don't you start with Lugh, because you busted him up good last time."

Isis leaves a quiet hall. Pierre locks himself in his study. Will bangs on the bathroom door, yelling at Coco to get out so he can piss. Torq has his back against the wall, arms folded across his chest. Fed up, Will leaves, threatening to urinate off the balcony. As soon as he's gone, Coco emerges from the bathroom, towel wrapped around her torso, hair dripping onto her freckled nose and shoulders. She gives Torq a bemused look. "I'm now dating those jets." She takes out her earbuds when she sees me and smiles. "You better be sticking around for the show, Evan. Pierre wrote me this new cadenza for 'We Forgot to Break Up' and we're going to premiere it tonight." She walks away, oblivious as usual.

Torq follows her, calling to me. "We leave in thirty minutes if you need a ride." The door slams in his face. He chooses another one.

Alone in the hall, I call out, "So, everyone's cool if I write about this, eh?"

Crickets.

I wait for them in the room with the fireplace and eventually decide it's a parlour.

Heidegger Stairwell played their first gig almost fifteen years ago on a beach in the middle of a forest in the Lake Huron hinterland to a congregation of drunken bushrats. Usually it doesn't feel that long ago, but sitting in the midst of an electrified crowd of sixteen thousand, most of whom smell like they're in high school, I'm feeling the years.

They're all up on the stage: Will at his kit, surrounded by toms and cymbals, a windchime tucked in the corner, djembe, goblet drums, timpani and bongos within reach; Pierre off to the side with his violin, bass or cello, or in the back directing an imported orchestra; Coco at the microphone with the concert harp, bass or assorted brass; Isis boxed in by a korg and a grand piano, a Bösendorfer tonight; Torq front stage, commanding attention with his acrobatic vocals and the poetry of his raw state; and finally, Lugh, off to the side, his virtuosity second fiddle to his brother's charisma, exactly how he'll want it.

All bathed, all styled, and away from the sick MacQueen baby and in the open air of idolatry, they seem happy, so I resent what Isis said. It's the music that keeps them together; not my machinations, such as they are. But the music's different than it used to be—so well rehearsed, every performance predictable. The melodies are there, the harmonies, the counterpoint, the surprising progressions, the inspired textures—they're communicating with the audience, but not with each other. Or with me.

The lights dim. Suddenly, that iconic guitar line with the lowered tuning on the seven-string guitar. And then ... Torq's high C that begins whisper-soft and grows to a war cry. The crunchy bass line, the syncopated low toms, the shivering strings. "One-Eyed Lugh," the first song they ever wrote as a band, after their first shared horror. And I can feel it, them—their frustrations channelled, the ecstasy of communal catharsis.

Most eyes are on Torq, although a good few are probably on Coco's breasts, which she'll be happy about these days. But I can't stop watching Lugh. He's wearing his Egyptian eyepatch, the one he got after Isis saved his life. It's his way of begging her to stay with them. I bet Isis would stay if Lugh actually asked. Although Evie didn't.

I slip out before the band finishes the encore so I don't get caught in the stampede. I bum a cigarette off a college-age backpacker loitering on the pavement; he's wearing Portland flannel and a beanie. The way he's looking at me, he must be a Heidegger fan, and what I'm seeing of him, he couldn't afford to get in the dome.

"You're not with the band are you?" he asks. He sounds American. South somewhere, I don't know.

I shake my head no.

"But you're like famous or something, right?"

Or something, I tell him.

He asks what I do. I tell him I'm a writer. Sort of. He seems to think that's glamorous because he's young and has a blog, which he feels is pertinent to the conversation. He says my face is familiar. He asks me if I'm on television. I say sometimes. He's embarrassed he can't place where he's seen me before. I don't tell him.

Instead, I give him the lanyard with my backstage pass and tell him to (respectfully) fawn over Isis Wong.

> I have no problem with this chapter. It seems as accurate a depiction as Evan will ever muster considering his slant world view.—**TORQ**

> As everyone will confirm, Evan made that fight up. Also, he could afford to be a little nicer in his descriptions of us.—**COCO**

> FYI, I knew Evie sent him.—**ISIS**

> if this is a gay harlequin im gonna flip to teh end.—**WILL**

Young Fogeys
THE EARLY DAYS

Let's talk about me, since that's why you're reading this book and not because it's pretending to be about one of the best-selling bands in the world. As illustrated by the last chapter, they grow up to be assholes anyway.

I was born in Emmet Lake Hospital on a scorching June afternoon. It was so hot my father, who paces even when he isn't nervous, slipped on a pool of my mother's sweat, knocked himself out and missed my birth. The tweety birds circling his head warned him I would be a handful.

My mother, the musician, screamed an E7, a semitone higher than her regular scream, and that was my cue. I waited in the wings fifteen hours, but hearing that strident wail I drew back the curtain to step onto the fluorescent-lit stage of life, clad in postmodern wardrobe of blood and placenta. Thus I was born, red and squealing; one large, dark-haired head, two blue eyes that would turn brown, one narrow nose, one weak jaw and pointed chin, a chickadee mouth, a narrow torso and long bowed legs. Five toes on one foot, six on the other—the doctors would remove the polydactylic digit hours after my birth and I would find out about the amputation when I was ten. Learning that I had been denied a flap of skin that looked like a sixth toe brought me the peace of self-understanding for roughly a day. Of course, the big gaping hole in my life wasn't the absence of a phalange, but I'm getting ahead of myself.

I was born Eva Jacklyn Strocker to Augusta (my mother) and Frank (my father, according to our identical chins). I grew up in a town north of Lake Huron called Emmet Lake—if you've heard of this town, you probably have a grandmother who retired there. If you've seen interviews with the band, you know they called me Evie.

And now, spoiler alert, they call me Evan.

Since 2005, at the entrance to Emmet Lake in Northern Ontario, just past the alien billboard, near the statue of the carbon atom masquerading as uranium, there is a plaque that reads:

> Home of Heidegger Stairwell
> Pierre Clowes Columba Coburn Lugh MacQueen
> Torquil MacQueen William Sacco Isis Wong
> They shine so bright because they drank the water.

Fact check: That plaque was taken down last year because of an E.coli outbreak. —**ISIS**

The joke is that locals glow in the dark because of the uranium deposits in the bedrock. But fans intent on pilgrimage needn't be alarmed: reports of toxic carcinogens in the water and above-average cancer rates (for Chernobyl) are vastly exaggerated.

Perceptive readers will note that I said nothing of plaques celebrating me. There are none. In fact, the Mayor of Emmet Lake has asked me on several occasions to stop associating myself with the town. Not because he's transphobic, no no no, but because he doesn't want my "sort of nonsense" associated with the town's good name. My sort of nonsense being everything I do and my entire personality. Actually, the Heritage Minister said something similar about my relationship with Canada. But, Emmet Lake is in Ontario and Ontario is in Canada, so the cat's out of the bag, sir.

Emmet Lake began as a mining outpost in the fifties, fuelled by the American nuclear procurement program. Pine, maple and bleached-bark birch went down to accommodate rows of prefabricated houses and dirt roads. For forty years the town boomed and busted until the last mine was shut down in the nineties. Miners headed out west and Emmet Lake became a resort settlement for retirees. The town developed a morbid population balance between the influx of retirees and their eternal exodus.

With a personnel changeover akin to McDonald's, Emmet Lake developed an environment of anonymity akin to city living. Lugh MacQueen used to jam with blues guitarist Bad-Breath Booker at the retirement centre, and this old Polish tenor who yelled all the time moulded Coco Coburn's larynx into an instrument of beauty. Of course, Heidegger's most important influence in my mind was my mother, Augusta Strocker, who taught music out of our bungalow. She instilled her love of melody in all the children who traipsed through her studio, including myself and the MacQueens.

Ah, the MacQueen boys. I'd be remiss if I didn't wax nostalgic about growing up across the street from Emmet Lake's most adored sons. Torquil Nathaniel MacQueen (yes that is his real name) was born in Emmet Lake in April, on Easter Sunday, almost fourteen months before me. That day the sun beamed, the snow melted, birds nested and the entire world waited expectantly. When Torq was born, the doctor fell to his knees and wept holy water, a chorus of nurses sang "Il est né le divin Enfant" in four-part harmony, and an angel descended from the heavens and said, "Lo, I bring tidings of great joy, for unto you is born the lead singer of Heidegger Stairwell, and he will be totally awesome, clever and a Generation Y sex symbol with swoon-worthy green eyes, perfect abdominals and elongated incisors. He will also look manly in pink. Praise him, for he will be vegan for you, and will give many women much pleasure with his mouth. Love him, for he will be a poet and will suffer great tragedies you will relate to but never face. Hail Torquil MacQueen."

Eleven months later, Lugh Gwydion MacQueen (also a real name) was born in Emmet Lake during a snowstorm. His mother almost didn't go to the hospital because she couldn't find the windshield brush. When Lugh was born, the doctor dropped him (Lugh landed on Doc's running shoe, didn't say boo), the nurses covered it up and the angel said, "And here is Torquil's brother. This one's kind of weird and quiet, so don't expect much and he may surprise you."

To explain their names I will say this: Mrs. MacQueen is a half-Quebecois, half-Ojibwa Medieval scholar turned industrial janitor who reads *The Lord of the Rings* every year. Her husband is very Scottish. Torq spent much of his life thinking Goodwill was a department store and he blames his father for this. He also spent much of his life thinking he was the only Torquil in the world until he discovered there were, like, five others, one being a singer, which sent him spiralling into a funk only cured by vegan ice cream and reading bad reviews on Pitchfork. He blames his mother for this because she assured him that he was the only one, which made living with the name bearable.

We are all pretty sure Lugh is the only Lugh in the world outside of the drunken hallucinations of Ancient Eire. Although apparently some fan named her baby for him. He wrote the kid a condolence letter.

From a young age the MacQueen boys were performers. They put on shows for their parents, who, after long days of Shop-Vaccing soupy old lady remains from bathtubs, liked nothing better than to lay on the couch and fall asleep listening to their sons' Teenage Mutant Ninja Turtle plays. But according to Lugh, he and his brother were dirty imps who spent all day wrestling in the mud with stray dogs, throwing rocks at bike kids and defacing hydrants with butt smiley faces. Sure, Lugh'd say, Torq forced him to do plays when they were young, and when they were older Lugh would strum the guitar and Torq would yell a song or dance or just wear his clothes backwards like Kris Kross. "But," he'd say, "We were bad." Remembering nine-year-old Torq screaming Weird Al's "My Bologna" into a carrot, I concur.

From the moment Lugh MacQueen got his first guitar, people knew there was something going on. That's people in general, which does not include Columba Coburn.

When Columba Miranda Coburn was born, the muses descended from Mount Olympus to bequeath upon her every artistic talent known to man, but Mrs. Coburn shooed them out of the delivery room since Coco was scheduled for a feeding and needed to focus. When they tried to sneak in later, she slapped them with

> We usually performed He-Man. I was He-Man and Lugh was my tiger. Then Evie came along and she was the tiger and Lugh was She-Ra.—**TORQ**

a restraining order. No one circumvented Mrs. Coburn's agenda.

> Are you kidding me?—**COCO**

Coco was a bubble child, treated simultaneously like an adult and a thoughtless homunculus. Kids made fun of her at school but she never noticed because she'd been trained to consider them feces-slinging baboons. Columba Coburn would be a perfectly moulded sculpture of enlightenment if her parents had their way. Except that Columba Coburn was a child, and by nature children sling shit. No one exemplified that like me.

The tweety birds warned my parents. My parents never warned others, though. Oh, Evie did what? Painted your couch green? Yes, that is her favourite colour. And she . . . dear me, she made your child ride a crazy carpet down the stairs? I suppose she is looking forward to winter. What's that, Officer? She stole our car to go to mini putting? That doesn't sound like her at all! My mother kept everything hush hush, as best she could in a town of sixteen thousand. As it was, every year there would be at least one kid who'd be pulled out of music lessons because of the terror of Evie Strocker. My mother never held it against me, though most other mothers gave me the stink eye at the mall.

Do I sound dissociated? I don't remember that much of being young; I only have the legends to go by, the anecdotes my mother hides behind. Me: Mom, Dad, I think I'm supposed to be a man. Mom: Evie, honey, do you remember that time we were in Sears when you pushed that mannequin over so you could change its clothes and its arm broke off and you decided to take it home so you put it in the bag with your dad's Dockers? I found it last week in the basement. Do you still want it?

My mother taught piano in the sunroom, which she called the conservatory, liking that the word did double duty. I usually sat nearby in the wood-panelled den, half-listening while I drew beards on my Barbies, or later, pictures of penises in my math homework. It was from my parent's floral sofa that I listened to Columba Coburn's piano lessons every Monday evening for eight years.

Columba was not a natural pianist; I overheard my mother say she lacked flexibility in her hands. But she took her music lessons seriously. Listening to fifty lessons of flubs a week, I knew even then this girl was the exception rather than the rule. I admired her, how she was always right and how good she looked in dresses. Columba wasn't especially pretty when she was young, with her unruly strawberry blond hair, broad nose and invisible eyebrows, but she acted like she was pretty and you believed her. She came to her lessons fifteen minutes early so we could play Sorry. At the time, I didn't know she wasn't allowed to play with other kids. Instead her days were scheduled with every type of activity available in small town Northern Ontario, including, but not limited to, piano lessons, singing lessons, acting lessons, choir, children's theatre, swimming lessons, skiing lessons, skating lessons, dance lessons, ringette, karate, dog training, catalogue modelling and probably Aristotelian philosophy and gun maintenance as well.

> Glib as ever. Someone is going to edit this, right?—**COCO**

That September evening was warm so my mother had the windows open. For most students it was torture listening to kids play in the street while you were trying to differentiate quarter notes from eighths. If she suffered, Columba didn't let on. But she wasn't a machine. Sounds of play may not have been distracting, but the amped up wails of a hockshop guitar tested her focus. My mother closed the window, which muted the sound, but after Columba nearly fainted from the heat (my father didn't believe in air conditioning), she flung it open again.

> It was from the Animal Rescue Charity Shop.—**TORQ**

Without a word, Columba got up from the piano, walked out of the sunroom, through the den and out the side door. Before my mother could protest, I jumped off the couch and followed Columba: through the garden, across the street to 63 Eden Crescent, through the rusty-hinged gate and into the backyard.

I didn't know the boys across the street—they went to the Catholic elementary school and didn't go outside. Their backyard was overgrown, full of goldenrod and berry bushes. There was an old oak with a broken tire swing, a dart board hanging on the fence, a rain-puckered ping pong table protected by scavenged picnic umbrellas, and one nine-year-old boy on the back porch, sitting on an amp playing a black guitar covered in Ninja Turtle

> the macqueens thought they were vampires until they were 12 cuz of there creepy teeth. tell evan to write that shit.—**WILL**

stickers who was presently told to shut up by a shrill little girl.

Lugh MacQueen, whose name I didn't know and wouldn't know how to spell for another three years, in an act of defiance against this trespasser, strummed the guitar tunelessly. Columba loosed a shrewish harangue: he was stupid, he didn't understand music, and he was wasting her parents' money by interrupting her piano lessons. She went on to insult his guitar, calling it a babyish piece of junk.

Neither Lugh nor Coco acknowledge this meeting; it's embarrassing for Coco, and Lugh doesn't do confrontation. But, knowing Lugh, Coco's rant could very well have precipitated his entire career.

> How would Evan remember that I said that? How would he remember anything we said? Does memoir mean "make up everything?" —COCO

Having never met this boy, I didn't know what he'd do; if he'd hit a girl, if he'd hit me, so I watched. But he never moved; he just shut down and looked at his shoes (orange Converse with a hole in the right toe box). Satisfied she'd solved the problem, Columba told me we were leaving. But the porch door opened.

Even at ten years old, Torquil MacQueen had that charisma only rock stars and despots seem to possess. If he was in a room, it was hard not to stare at him. It wasn't his looks, although even then, dressed in ripped jeans and a mustard-stained Kresge t-shirt, he was striking. Looking back on photos of the MacQueen brothers, they were almost identical when young, save for Torq's hair, which he'd grown in deference to his Ojibwa grandfather. Yet people never noticed Lugh.

"Did you just scream at my brother?" He let the storm door crack shut behind him.

"He's annoying everyone in the neighbourhood," said Columba.

Torq said something like, "And your screaming isn't?"

She gawped, not used to being called out. "I only screamed because he wouldn't stop playing."

"I'd rather listen to him play than you scream."

Despite never acknowledging the quarrel, Lugh remembered this exchange well enough years later. After the "accidental" leak of Torq and Coco's sex tape in 2009, YouTube became saturated with remixes and mashups of Coco's sexual vocalizing.

This shed a different light on Lugh's statement to *Esquire* in 2007. When asked about his nighttime practice schedule and the noise complaints he often received, sometimes from his own brother, Lugh commented, "He said he'd rather listen to me play than her scream." ←

> Trivia: Lugh based his guitar solo in "Forgot to Come for You" on Coco's sex screams. —**ISIS**

But even as a kid, Coco didn't know how to deal with childish low blows. In shy support I whispered to her, "Who cares what he wants, he smells like garbage and cat pee."

And she said, loudly, "Yeah, nobody gives a care what you want. You stink like garbage and cat pee." In our defence, there were two litter boxes and a bag of garbage on the far end of the porch.

"Who *are* you?" He sauntered toward us. I was both afraid and hopeful for a fight.

"Columba Miranda Coburn," she said.

He chuckled. "*Columba*."

"It means dove. What's your name?"

"Torquil."

I giggled. "Dorkwill."

"What's that? Dorkwill?" Columba jeered.

"Like I never heard that. Try again, Co Co." He smirked. "Coco. Sounds like a poodle."

Columba wasn't used to being teased, either. So she pushed him. Caught off guard, he fell, knocking over trays of kitty litter, popping open the bag of garbage. Lugh stepped out the way.

Columba came up with this gem: "Dorkwill, Dorkwill, garbage man, smells like pee and an old trash can!" She turned to me, expectantly. "Well? You gotta sing it too, right?"

So I yelled along. Torq stood. The song caught in Columba's throat and she bolted. Torquil took off after her, visible stink waves wafting behind him. I was left in the backyard with Lugh.

"Your guitar is cool." I said and ran.

Torq had Columba pinned in the grass, rubbing his garbage and urine-stained shirt all over her. She vacillated between shrieking and laughing, half-heartedly trying to kick him off or bite his forearms.

Lugh came over and watched with me from the path. "You live across the street, right?" he said.

"Yeah. I'm Strocker. Evie."

"Lou MacQueen. Are you a boy or a girl?"

I paused. "I'm a boy."

"No you're not. You're a girl. Stop it Dorkwill!" Columba shrieked as Torq rubbed his shirt in her face.

Lugh said, "Why did you say you're a boy?"

I asked if he was mad.

He shrugged. "You think my guitar's cool."

The week after the incident Columba Coburn came into her piano lesson and told my mother to call her Coco. When she said that, she didn't know Torq and Lugh were in our kitchen playing 52 Pickup because her mother had reported the MacQueens to Children's Aid for leaving the nine-year-old to babysit the eight-year-old. In the MacQueens' defence, they thought Torq was mature for his age. In Mrs. Coburn's defence, he wasn't. So my mother became their afterschool babysitter, and they became mine, because, as you've likely surmised, I was a burgeoning personality disorder. And after I tricked a winter-chilled Lugh into getting in the dryer and chopped off Torq's chieftain hair while he was sleeping, Torq and his hegemonic aspirations suppressed my revolution, first with headlocks, then cookies, and then charm.

My mother thought they'd be good for me, since I was always so quiet, even when I was bad, which I was most of the time. I found my shrill voice yelling at the MacQueens to get the heck off my couch, or to stop eating my Corn Pops, or to beat this durn Bowser for me, or to go with me to the mini putt, or to steal a car with me to go to the mini putt. They talked me out of amazing schemes, which they should regret, and then made me play keyboard in their faux band, which consisted of butchering Aerosmith or Guns N' Roses. It would have been cooler to pretend we were Indiana Joneses, but whatever. I was never afraid of anything when I was with them because to them everything was possible, even becoming rock stars with a three-string guitar and a voice like microphone feedback.

> Take that out. And for the record, my mother did not report the MacQueens. That was Old Mrs. Scheck with the garden gnomes Evan defaced and blamed on Torq. —**COCO**

Insert here a montage of two boys and one questionable in pack formation prowling the mean streets of small-town Northern Ontario, brawling in pick-up road hockey games, launching neighbourhood-wide Super-Soaker wars, watching newly released movies on the TVs at Zellers, growing taller and manlier, yes even me, at adequate adolescent increments. The soundtrack is a mash-up of MC Hammer and Nirvana with some Ace of Base thrown in because it was the only CD my parents owned for a year.

Now skip to disc six in your totally cool multiple CD player. This is also the amount of years we will leap. What's playing? Green Day's *Dookie*: the album that wore out the laser on Will Sacco's Discman.

If our jam sessions count, the yet unnamed Heidegger Stairwell was formed in 1989. However, the band usually agrees that Heidegger Stairwell began in 1994 when Torq and Lugh MacQueen formed a bad power trio with Will Sacco.

When William Robert Sacco was born, the delivery room was full of screaming gremlins because his mother already had seven boys. Will's older brothers dropkicked his fairy godmother in the head, which left a door open for a sloth demon to sneak in and shack up in Will's forebrain.

> evan cant use the wrd sloth demon unless he pays me a million dolars—I TMed that shit.—**WILL**

Will was my first nemesis, the deviant who threw a baseball at my head and put me in the hospital with a concussion when I was thirteen. And, of course, the future drummer of Heidegger Stairwell.

When I played baseball or soccer I wasn't "a girl," which athletes don't think is sexist but is always used as a putdown. No, I was always just Evie. On the field, you're only as respected as your performance. And I was good—taller than lots of the boys, stronger than some, and faster than most. I didn't mind people looking at me as much when I was in uniform, because everyone wore the same uniform—we were all the same. (Except the other, actual, girl, who wasn't the same because she played like a girl.)

That girl was different in other ways too, since at fourteen she started to fill out the uniform. After that, "girl" was still an insult on the field but not so much in the dugout. The day she

> i was itchin to go after Ev cuz at our last tournamant he put a chocolat bar on the bench just as I sat down. people thought I crapped myself. fuckhead did it on purpos.—**WILL**

got her water bra was the day my teammates noticed I was also supposed to be a girl, even though there was no curve to my hips and my chest was concave like a starving African kid on those exploitative beggarmercials. Will had been itching to go after me since I won shortstop over him. So, after practice, Will and some guys waited for me to get out of the girls' changeroom, which was really just the public washroom. The catcher held my arms while Will positioned one of his mother's huge Wonderbras over my shirt and stuffed it with gravel. Will had a sixth sense about how to torture people, because there were few things I found more embarrassing than women's underwear, especially in relation to my body.

"Look at the tranny!" said Will, honking the breasts he'd made me. That was the first time someone called me that. I didn't know what it meant so, since this was pre-Google, I went home and asked my mother. Mom: Tranny? Like a transformer? Oh, honey, do you remember that time you decided you wanted to be a robot so you went to the neighbours' garage, the Bronsons you know, and took their old boxes for your costume, but you just left everything you emptied all over the garage floor and Mr. Bronson drove over his mother-in-law's urn?

Up till then, the technicality of being a girl hadn't properly registered for me. People told me I was a girl, but I didn't know what that meant besides liking pink, which I didn't, or having long hair, which I didn't, but Torq did and they said he was a boy so I figured that was negotiable. Breasts scared me though. I knew they were powerful because my dad, who normally took pride in not watching commercials, didn't change the TV channel when there was a big-breasted woman selling something. I was relieved not to have them. They seemed unwieldy.

I found another old G-cup bra hanging out of my locker the next day. I threw it in the trash but Will fished it out and hunted me down after first period and hung it on my packsack while I wasn't looking. I didn't notice until I'd walked the entire school. By that time, people had started to call me 42G. In those days I think my chest was a 32AAA.

Lugh, who after years at Catholic school had finally been integrated into reality, took the bra. He held it over his chest, which was broader than mine and was still dwarfed by the silky underthing, and asked, wry, if it was mine. After school, Will and his entourage followed us to the field we crossed to get home. Will pushed Lugh from behind, demanding he give back the bra.

Lugh donned it again, fastening it all by himself. Will said everyone would know Lugh was a tranny (that word again!) if he didn't give us back the bra. Lugh was Zen, standing in the middle of the field wearing a droopy Wonderbra over his Mondetta t-shirt, which enraged Will enough to punch him in the chest.

The humiliation had been boiling up all day and I wanted nothing more than for Lugh to beat the shit out of this guy. Instead, he shook Will's hand and whispered something in his ear. Will looked over at me, eyes wide, Adam's apple bobbing in his swarthy throat. In his most amiable voice, Lugh told me to walk. Will may not have been worth Lugh's effort, but he was worth mine, so when Lugh tried to herd me, I ducked under his arm and ran for Will. I called out "hey!" and he turned around just in time for my fist to connect with his eye socket. Lugh grabbed me around the waist and ran, me under his armpit like a football.

I'm not saying I was scared of Will Sacco, but I played hooky for the next three days. Upon my return, I flinched at shadows, ducked into bathrooms, hid behind fat teachers, waiting for Will to exact his vengeance. He was sporting a solid shiner, purple from the corner of his close-set eye to the top of his cheekbone. I knew I was in for it.

At the end of the day, I figured he'd be waiting for me at the chain-link by the field, so I ducked out the gym door. I ran right into Will's cronies. They corralled me by the track, calling me 42G. One of them said he thought my tits were growing and gave me a purple nurple, telling the rest them it was like trying to grab a freckle. They all grabbed a freckle.

My voice shaking, I said I'd break their noses if they didn't leave me alone. Then I slipped away and ran. I didn't get far before one of them got hold of my packsack and jerked me onto my ass. Slipping my arms out of the straps, I scrambled to my feet and ran headlong into Will Sacco and his NOFX shirt.

"Watch where you're going, Strocker." He grabbed my biceps. I remembered Lugh saying to never make eye contact with unpredictable animals, so I kept my head down.

"The hell's with you?" said Will.

"I'm waiting for you to kick my ass."

"Tch. I'm not gonna beat up a chick, even if she is crazy."

"Your friends were . . . " I didn't want to say it; I didn't want to draw more attention to my body. It was disgusting how everyone was focused on a body part I didn't have and didn't want.

"Friends?" said Will. "Those guys are tools. You wanna beat the shit out of them with me?"

I blinked.

"Suit yourself." He turned to his ex-buddy. "Yo, the backpack, asshole."

"Hey, Will, we were just . . . "

Will downed the guy with one punch to the jaw. "Yeah, I saw what you were doing."

It was bad timing—a gym teacher was walking to his car and saw Will KO the bastard. He was suspended for three weeks.

I delivered Will's homework at the end of each week. He lived a few streets over, in a two-storey near the skating pond. Lugh walked with me. I didn't ask him to; I didn't even tell him where I was going. He sat on the green electrical box in the Saccos' yard and waited.

Will's father let me in. He was bald, barrel-chested and a bank manager. His wife was a homemaker whose full-time job was cleaning up after her nine children, of whom Will was the second youngest.

Will had a room in the basement. The walls were covered with posters of punk bands, swords and sorcery art and swimsuit models. When I arrived, Will was sitting behind a drum kit, a Sears special with a couple of toms, an undersize bass drum and one high hat.

"What do you want?"

"I have your homework." I placed it on his desk.

"I'm on holidays." He smashed the cymbal. "Whatever. Thanks."

"You punched that guy for me."

"I punched that guy because I wanted to." Will tried a drum roll and dropped his sticks. Swearing, he kicked over the cymbal.

"Nice kit." It was junk but I didn't know any better.

"My mom says I have anger problems. I'm supposed to hit the drum when I get pissed."

"Are you pissed at me?"

"I just like the drums. Especially the bass. Listen." He hit the pedal twice, once hard, once soft. "Sounds like a heartbeat, eh?"

"So you weren't sticking up for me?" I wanted to know what made this guy tick.

"You can take care of yourself. Exhibit A." He pointed to his fading black eye with the drum stick.

"You were a jerk to me," I said, defensive.

"Everyone's a jerk to everyone."

It didn't make any sense. "What did Lugh MacQueen say to you?"

Will turned red. "He's a good friend, isn't he?" Will looked me over. "It's better you don't need a bra. Those things are hard to undo."

I was so tired of people talking about breasts that I failed to notice he was hitting on me. I stormed out and got halfway home before realizing I'd left Lugh behind.

The second week I found Will playing along with his Mötley Crüe album, getting about a quarter of the beats in. He told me he had a dream about me wearing a miniskirt and killing zombies. I told him I didn't believe in skirts and that his room smelled like a toilet. Will said I should wear a miniskirt because I had long legs and it would be sexy. I told him I'd never shaved my legs and asked him if that was sexy. He asked me if he could shave my legs. I kicked over his cymbal.

The third week I dropped off his homework we made out on his desk. I let him touch my chest, my ass, but kicked him when he pawed between my legs. I told him Torq and Lugh were trying to form a band and needed a drummer. Will said he'd do whatever I wanted if he could just stick it in a little. He still joined the band even though I said no.

The band, such as it was, met at Will's to practice. They played Nirvana, KISS, Aerosmith and the Beatles. After an hour Torq would usually leave to meet some girl. That left Will, Lugh and me to pound back a two-four and play drunken Dungeons and Dragons. When we were good and sloshed, Lugh usually slipped out and left Will and I alone. We lost our virginity after vanquishing a red dragon.

Our relationship disintegrated after that. We never broke up, we just evolved to friends who fucked, then just friends, and finally band members. There was no delineation and no hard feelings.

Sound familiar? That would be the inspiration for the song "We Forgot to Break Up."

Initially the band wasn't called Heidegger Stairwell—they were called the Young Fogeys. They were a run-of-the-mill garage band for a year and a half. They got their first gig in 1997 and were paid ten bucks, which almost covered their gas.

> that hippie reminded me we al feel the same pain, blah blah blah—**WILL**

> Lugh told Will what we always told guys who wanted to kill Evie: that he should be nice to her because she gave the best blow jobs in town.—**TORQ**

I'm still wondering what Lugh said to Will that day in the field.

38 KAYT **BURGESS**

One-Eyed Lugh
MAY 1997

In Celtic mythology, the god Lugh Lámhfhada knocks out his grandfather Balor's evil third eye with a sling. In Heidegger mythology, it was Lugh's eye, his right one.

Fans have always been fascinated by Lugh's eyepatch. For months after the first CD came out, hipster teens wore graphic patches as fashion statements. In 2005, Heidegger Stairwell came under attack by the Ophthalmologists of America for inspiring young people with good eyesight to limit their vision by wearing them. In answer, Lugh came out, allowing himself to be photographed without the patch. The fascination escalated, culminating with the photo spread in *Vogue* showcasing eyepatch designs and fetishizing Lugh's scarred eye socket.

> Fact check: This was one ophthalmologist in some obscure journal.—ISIS

> Fact check: Not *Vogue*.—ISIS

Much of the fascination has been attributed to his refusal to discuss the incident. Rumours circle the internet, ranging from a drunken fistfight with Will to serving in special ops to syphilis and a half-million other theories. The reality of it wasn't so dramatic.

It happened at the band's first gig.

A half hour north of Emmet Lake there's a secluded beach off one of the old mining roads where the kids used to party. We'd build a bonfire, pitch tents, drink Mooseknuckle and pass around the most emaciated joints ever rolled. That May two-four weekend Will, Lugh, Isis Wong and I squished into Will's hatchback and joined society in the wilderness.

This marked the first time I'd hung out with Isis Wong. Sure, I'd gone to birthday parties and school events with *Isa* Wong, but I didn't know Isis, who had changed her name and bleached her hair white. The first time I saw the new her I thought she was a foreign exchange student; she looked like she belonged on *Sailor Moon* with her ass-long platinum-blond hair and bitch boots. Girls called her a slut behind her back, sometimes to her face, and, according to the guys, they all got with her. The joke was on them, because Isis Wong is gay.

Isa came out to her parents the summer before she changed her name. She went to camp, fell in love with a counsellor, lost her virginity, had her heart broken, and came back Isis. Her parents, who moved from Hong Kong to Toronto, then Emmet Lake, owned the electronics shop in the mall. Apparently they took the news rather well, especially her father, who thought it meant Isis would stay a virgin forever. She never brought guys home, even friends, lest her father take away her Lesbian Freedom.

> Ev forgot to write what hapened when isis was born. Something about chinese ancesters and dragons and angry man hating lesbo banshees. —**WILL**

I'd found Isis fascinating ever since her makeover, but never had any reason to approach her. She hung around with Coco and Pierre Clowes, a flamboyant violinist who drove two hours twice a week to play with the symphony orchestra in the city. All three of them were classical musicians, trained multi-instrumentalists who talked nothing but opera, concertos and symphonies. So I don't know how I ended up on her radar, but one day in the hall at school she slid her arm through mine. I immediately went on guard, expecting her to try to humiliate me (as I would have done). Instead she said, "We look super hot together, don't you think?"

I said something about not being able to see us because I was part of us. I never felt hot—I was gangly, I slouched. My hair was nondescript brownness and full of dandruff. I had whiteheads on my forehead and acne on my back. I sort of looked like a girl, which always surprised me when I caught myself in the mirror.

Isis came to the lake for the long weekend. She lied to Coco and Pierre about going away with her parents for the weekend and told her parents to lie for her as well. We picked her up on the way out to the lake, Lugh and Will in the front, Isis and me in the back.

Will was nervous around Isis—he was one of the guys on the wrestling team who'd said he got with her. I could see him sweating in the rearview, and he kept jacking up the air-conditioning, even though the rest of us were freezing our asses off. I suppose he could've been nervous because the Young Fogeys were going to perform for the first time that night. But it was probably Isis; she has that affect on people.

One of Torq's friends brought generators so the band could power their amps and mics at the lake. Will routinely destroyed his drums so his kit was never complete and that night he brought a patched-up bass drum, a snare and the small set of bongos he stole from the elementary school years earlier. (Note: Now that I am confessing on his behalf, perhaps he will gift the school with a new set.)

We set up near the bonfire. Someone said Torq was with his girlfriend of the week so the Fogeys would have to wait to play. Lugh and I sat at the bonfire while Will joined his wrestling buddies to drink beer through a pool noodle and Isis helped at the barbeque.

"What's the deal with you and Isis?" said Lugh.

I told him I didn't know what he was talking about. He shrugged, didn't qualify. I probably sighed. "What do you mean?"

"Are you, like, a lesbian now?"

It took me off guard. "Why?"

Lugh has a special intimate smile for secrets. His right canine slips out between his lips and he snorts a little. "Why do you think?"

"Because Isis is a lesbian," I deadpanned and Lugh mouthed along with me. He waggled his eyebrows.

I caught Isis's eye at the grill. She held up a hamburger in one hand and a hotdog in the other and offered one, then the other. That subtext wasn't lost on me. Lugh laughed.

"It's not funny."

"Is."

I hadn't given him an answer about being a lesbian. Truth was, I didn't have one. I didn't know what I was back then. I liked being around men, and enjoyed the look, smell and taste of their bodies. But the one time I slept with Will had traumatized me. If I hadn't matured so much over the last few years, I'd blame him just to be a dick. But it had nothing to do with his "mad bedroom skillz." Everything about him had been so comfortable, familiar. I understood his body better than mine. But having him in me, it felt like he'd opened a wound and shoved himself in. I'd held it together just long enough to get home before being sick. After that I just went down on him.

So maybe I was a lesbian. I never felt like I belonged with other women, but maybe that was how lesbians felt. In the back of my mind I knew that wasn't right, but in the foreground I knew *I* wasn't quite right. Even when I was at home, in my room, the safest place in the world, it was like I was orphaned inside my own skin.

"Just because I hang out with a lesbian doesn't make me a lesbian," I mumbled, looking for an out. "Will's setting up. We should help him."

"Yeah, Torq'll be done soon enough. He doesn't usually fuck for more than two songs."

I don't always remember everything perfectly, even with the help of journals, post-its and recordings, but Lugh MacQueen did say that, and has said it since, although as far as I know now, Torquil MacQueen is up to fucking for five or six songs.

> I fuck for entire albums now.—**TORQ**

> He usually fucks for three and falls asleep on top of you.—**COCO**

I wasn't going to let Torq get out of set up—he was as lazy then as he is now. So I unzipped the tent door and poked my head in. It reeked like piss and honey inside.

"Hey! I thought we were having a threesome," I yelled. "Thanks for waiting."

The random blonde saw me and squealed. My work was done.

Torq helped build the makeshift stage on the beach from fronds and pine branches.

They checked their levels. The concert started just as the sun was going down.

By this time, the band had started to refine their sound to a fairly commercial alternative rock outfit, with hints of blues, world music and folk. Torq was into Queen, David Bowie, Joy Division, Beach Boys, the Beatles (but only stoner songs) and Lugh chain-smoked Zeppelin, Pink Floyd, Van Halen, Robert Johnson, and had a hard-on for the Canadian band The Tea Party. Will was still on his pop punk kick and he'd had to buy *Dookie* three times since Lugh kept breaking the CD. But they didn't sound like any of those bands: they just sounded like every other garage band. Other than Lugh, the Young Fogeys lacked the musicality and skill to get the sound they imagined.

I watched them play from the edge of the beach, the surf lapping around my feet. In the gloaming, with the bass drum pulsing and Torq's tenor throaty and rasping, the scene came across as primal, a pagan ritual.

"They're decent," said Isis, coming up from behind me, leaning her chin on my shoulder. "Drummer's a Neanderthal, but he can keep a beat. Torq's got something—range, sure, and that tone is so different. But it's more. Presence. Charisma. Sensuality. Fuck, magic."

"And Lugh?" Lugh was my best friend; he was the one I wanted her approval for.

"Brother's gifted. He could be a concert guitarist someday if he wanted."

I puffed with pride and wondered what it was he did want. He never talked about the future, never the past; he only made wry comments on the moment.

"You're fucking him aren't you?"

Isis never pulls punches—she fit right in that way. "I told you, we broke up."

"Not Will. Baby MacQueen."

She sounded so serious I had to laugh. "Lugh doesn't do girls; he only does music." The guitar cradled in his arms, pressed to his hips, his focus completely on the instrument, I'm sure everyone could see it was his first love and always would be.

"They could use a keyboardist, you know."

I looked back at her. Her black eyes were full of bonfire. "You offering?"

"Only if they're looking. I don't deal well with rejection." She winked, but she wasn't joking. I hoped this wasn't supposed to be subtextual.

"I'll check. Subtly."

After they finished both sets, Lugh settled into strumming Eric Clapton and B.B. King on a boulder near the bonfire. I saddled up beside. He asked if I had a request.

"Come as You Are."

His fingers flickered lightly over the guitar neck, picking out the Nirvana song's opening riff. There were some scattered claps of approval.

"You guys sounded good tonight."

"Cool."

"But it's missing something."

"Missing a lot," he agreed.

"What about a keyboard?"

He nodded. "We're missing that."

"You want one?"

He didn't answer me for a moment, playing deep through the bridging solo, eyes closed, head bobbing with the rhythm. When he returned to the verse pattern, he looked over at me. "This about your girlfriend?"

"She's not my—"

"Is Isis offering to be our keyboardist?"

"Only if you want one. If you don't, then she's not."

"I'll ask the guys." He finished the song and started in on "All Along the Watchtower." It wasn't quite the version Heidegger would include on the *War Song* special edition, but it was a prototype. "Should I ask them if they want a clarinet player too?"

I played the clarinet for five minutes when I was fourteen. "I'm going to punch you in the face."

"Then I won't be able to play and there'll be no band for your girlfriend."

"You think an awful lot of yourself, Lugh MacQueen."

"Naw, just the right amount."

A game of tackle flared up on the other side of the bonfire. People headed into the water, and there were half a dozen streakers, their winter-white asses jiggling after a long hibernation. Torq had disappeared, probably into a tent, and Isis was amusing herself by manipulating wrestlers into fighting each other on the beach.

A drunken volleyball guy—Mike Something—wandered up to Lugh in an inebriated zigzag. "Can you play Offspring?"

Lugh: Offspring. Tch. "No, man, sorry."

"Yeah, they're kinda hard. How 'bout Weezer?"

Lugh loved Weezer, mostly because they referred to Dungeons and Dragons in one of their songs. He offered up the opening to "Say It Ain't So" and Mike Something whooped and sang along, out of key.

All the drunks congregated around the fire, singing Weezer like Nike-shoed satyrs at a sausagefest bacchanalia. I even joined in, which I never did it because the femininity in my voice disoriented me.

Mike's buddy threw his unopened beer bottle in the fire.

When the bottle exploded, I saw Lugh's hand go up and I felt a stinging in my neck, on my chest. My t-shirt was wet. I touched the sting and cut my finger on the shard of glass embedded just below my collarbone. That's when I saw the guitar on the ground in front of me. Lugh wasn't there. He'd been sitting on the rock right beside me.

I turned to see him on the ground, curled up, his hand over his eye, his fingers bloody. As pale as he usually was, his skin was grey.

"Lugh?" I don't know if I whispered or yelled. "Lugh, what's wrong?" I wanted to crawl down to him, but I was afraid to move. My shirt was soaked and I didn't know if I should take out the glass or if I would bleed out. I had watched too many doctor shows.

"I'm bleeding. My eye's bleeding... I can taste it. Blood's in my mouth."

He kept saying that: the blood was in his mouth. Suddenly I

found a voice, that shrill one I didn't understand, but I worked it like a siren, yelling for help, for Torq, for Will, for anyone.

"What the hell's going on?" Isis ran over, stopped a foot away, and swore.

"Lugh's face is bleeding," I said. "His eyes. They're bleeding. And his mouth."

"Holy fuck." She threw up. Isis wasn't drunk.

"Should I take it out?" It was like a stalagmite growing from my chest.

Wiping her mouth, Isis pulled off her shirt and handed it to me, telling me to wrap it around the base of the glass in my chest to stop the bleeding, but gently. She carefully took the shard out of my neck. Then bent down to check on Lugh.

"Oh my god."

Someone, somewhere asked where the music had gone.

"Isis? Is Lugh okay?"

"I need keys. Where is that piece of shit Will Sacco?" Isis stormed the beach, screaming for Will. She waded into the water to yell at the swimmers, who just cheered for her shirtlessness, and then checked the tents. She emerged from the big blue one with a naked and half-erect Torq. Throwing his clothes in his face, she pointed at us and disappeared into the woods. Sobering, Torq pulled his legs through his pants. He saw us and the coloured drained from his liquor-reddened face. Torq crawled to his brother's side, calling him Louie-Louie, Louie-Louie.

Isis ran out of the woods with a set of keys dangling from her hands and Will on her tail, swearing.

"Help Torq get Lugh in the car. Here you go, Evie, nice and slow." She half-carried me to Will's car and put me in the front seat. Will scratched at his gelled hair.

"Shit, they're gonna bleed all over it."

"Then go get some blankets!" Isis snapped, calling him a fucktard as he left. Will returned with a blanket for the back seat, one for Lugh, and one for me, for which I was thankful. May isn't warm in Northern Ontario, even when you have all your blood.

Isis helped Torq and Lugh into the backseat. Lugh was drifting in and out of consciousness. She closed their doors and mine. Will went for the driver's seat but she pushed him aside and climbed in.

"Bitch, that's my car!" He yelled and drunkenly kicked the tire of said car.

Isis rolled down the window. "You're goddamn wasted, Will Sacco. If you think I'm going to let you drive them to the hospital you're out of your mind. Sober up and take Torq's car home. Have his girl too, for all I care—I bet she won't even notice she's being mauled by a hairy gorilla." She turned on the ignition. "And FYI, Will, I'm a lesbian."

She tore down the mining road. When she hit the highway, she floored it, as though she had sirens.

I received three stitches on my neck and nineteen on my chest. Emmet Lake General kept me overnight, a first since Will Sacco had put me in the hospital with a concussion. They called my parents, who rushed in at three a.m., jackets over pyjamas. My mother had face-mask goop in her eyebrows.

Once Lugh was stable, they flew him to the city. He came back to school a week later, wearing an eyepatch emblazoned with the eye of Horus.

"A tribute to our little mother, Isis," he said. When I told Isis in music class, she openly wept and the teacher had me take her into the practice room.

"And you know what else?" I said to her after she'd regained her composure. "The guys want you in the band."

"Even Will?" She grimaced. "I did steal his car, call him a fucktard and publically humiliate him."

"Especially Will." Will didn't even remember any of that, except the car.

And it was true. His exact words when I brought up Isis were: "Hell yeah. If I ever get famous and O.D. on crack or heroin or whatever weird shit they cook up by then, I want that dyke there. I don't trust any of you assholes to save my life."

Tell Evan to take that out.—**TORQ**

Confidence, Man
JUNE 1997

A word-for-word transcription of a Young Fogeys jam session circa 1997:

ISIS: This song is illiterate. These chord progressions are boring. What are you assholes actually trying to say? What does this band even mean?
TORQ: It's all about the music, babe.
WILL: Music isn't about anything. It just sounds good.
ISIS: Music is about communicating. Emotions and stories. It's not just patterned sound. Or, in your case, chaos.
WILL: Would you shut your carpetmuncher?
ISIS: No. You need to learn how to manipulate sound so it affects people how you want. But you don't even know the difference between a major and minor chord so why am I bothering?
 (Lugh plays a G major chord into an A minor.)
 (End recording. Evie has fallen asleep on the sofa and does not turn over the tape.)

And now a hypothetical transcription of a Heidegger Stairwell song-writing session circa 2009:

TORQ: Guys, I just came up with the world's most beautiful melody. Listen and it will blow your minds.
PIERRE: That melody is derivative.

ISIS: What does that melody mean?

TORQ: It's an exquisitely crafted vehicle for the lyrics, which are right here. Listen.

PIERRE: Those lyrics are derivative.

ISIS: No, what does the melody communicate outside the lyrics?

TORQ: Just listen and you'll feel it.

ISIS: Torquil, I want to understand the concept behind it so I can ensure the piano works thematically.

WILL: Who gives a shit? Let's just fucking play something, already.

TORQ: Everyone shut up and listen to me. I command you to listen to my beautiful music, peons. ← *Droll.—***TORQ**

ISIS: Fine. Torq can recite poetry and Will can rap a tap tap his twigs against the wall and we'll call that a song. And our fans will snap their fingers, drop acid and engage in an orgy inspired by art for art's sake.

*their should b comma-things or something cuz that is word fer fuckin word.—***WILL**

*Fact: That is a direct quote.—***ISIS**

(Lugh plays the Mario Brothers theme.)

COCO: *(Looks up from her opera magazine.)* Lugh, is that the new song? Do I have a part? ←

*I don't know what he's implying here, but I've written songs on every album. I don't just sit around mooching like someone.—***COCO**

So let's remember 1997, the year Lugh lost his eye, the Fogeys wrote their first song, I was suspended for dressing like a school shooter and Torq's charmed life was rattled by unrequited love. Also, I experimented with lesbianism. Conveniently for this book, most of that happened around the same time.

The Young Fogeys changed after trading Lugh's eye for Isis's keys. Before, they had just been a group of guys channelling their small-town frustrations into shallow covers of bad songs by good bands. But Isis was an aficionado, a classical pianist and second-generation Chinese-Canadian. She was always telling me how her mother accused her of being lazy, but the boys were intimidated by her discipline and called her Dragon Lady, sometimes to her face. I told Torq that was racist; he said it wasn't racist if she called herself that too. ←

*Correction: I said it once. And, FYI, it's still racist.—***ISIS**

In May 1997, after the latest in a long line of worldwide school shootings, our high school enforced a policy that banned people from dressing entirely in black. I was the first one in the school sent home for looking like a mass murderer. The VP said I wasn't allowed back until I injected some colour in my life. Feeling similar about his life choices, I spray-painted his Honda lime green. That was over ten years ago, so I believe I can invoke the statute of limitations.

My parents grounded me, but it was hardly enforced. No one tossed Torq when he burst into my house that afternoon, nearly barrelling over my father who stood at the door waiting for the newspaper. My mother even invited Isis inside when she showed up at the door claiming she'd given Torq a ride home and he'd stolen the keys out of her ignition.

We found Torq in the sunroom at my mother's piano. He wanted us to listen to a song. Isis said she was tired of listening to him. He told us it was a song he had written, but he was shy when he said it. It wasn't done, he said, but he wanted Isis to tell him her honest opinion.

Torq had changed after the incident at the lake. Although he was older, he'd always been the less responsible of the brothers. When Lugh came home from the hospital, Torq became his nursemaid. At the beginning, he refused to accept that Lugh's eye was gone, and he read up on surgeries, transplants. Torq, not Lugh, had a breakdown when the doctor told them Lugh would never see out of that eye again. Torq, with Will in tow, had tried to track down the idiot who threw the bottle in the fire. I'm glad they never found him. Torq would've killed him.

He feels too much. Of everything. And that was never more evident than when he sang what would become "One-Eyed Lugh." It was unstructured, the lyrics clumsy and esoteric, like a Doors or Alanis Morissette parody, but it sent a shiver through you. Once Isis made sense of the tune, she improvised, his 1-4-6 chords getting a blues drop and a *tierce de Picardy*. They ran it twice without stopping. Torq rasped out the end of the song. My parents clapped from the kitchen.

The quiet moment following was loud with expectation. Torq stood over Isis, face flushed, hands shaking: with anxiety, with touches of the performance mania he'd come to be known for.

> I see Evan omitted the Black = Murderer picket. Idiot. I had to tell all three of the black guys about Evie's BJs or they would've killed her. I forgot about the one girl. She kicked Evie's inadvertently racist ass. —**TORQ**

> it was jason petrosian. he got wasted after graduation and confesed. i didn't tell Torq cuz he woulda fucked that guy up royally. evie and i beat up his car with shovels that nite. —**WILL**

Isis studied the lyrics, smoothing out the paper that had been crumpled in his pocket for days.

"It needs work," she said, "but it's good. It's *something*."

Torq smiled with relief, showing the full glory of those incisors.

Isis said, "But it's too hard for you."

"I wrote it. For me to sing."

Isis handed him the song. "And you can't sing it. Listen to yourself—you just blew out your voice. You don't have those notes."

"Yes I do. I just hit them."

Isis was firm. "They're not usable. You'd never pull that off at a gig."

He looked like he was going to hit her. Instead he threw himself onto the sofa beside me, defeated.

"Better yet, you could get some singing lessons," said Isis. "You keep hollering like you do, you're not going to have any voice in ten years."

Torq grumbled, said he knew how to sing already.

Isis laughed. "Spewing sustained sound isn't singing. There's supposed to be technique and artistry. Look, there's this crazy Polish guy who teaches Coco—I could get his number for you."

"Coco Coburn sings?"

Isis asked him if he lived under a rock.

I walked Isis to her truck, telling her all about the injustice I'd faced that day, the fashion martyr that I was. She climbed into the driver's seat, swinging her naked legs under the wheel. I caught myself wondering what they would feel like.

"I wax," she said. "That's why they aren't prickly. You've never shaved your legs before have you? Do you need someone to show you how?"

I told her no, embarrassed that Will told her about my legs. Or Torq. Or Lugh, even—they all teased me about my fuzzy ankles. Isis's smooth legs were pretty, but I didn't want them on my body.

She pushed my hair out of my face. The gesture felt very intimate.

"You need a haircut," she said. And, because she was on a roll: "And you can't wear those clothes anymore—those jeans are too short, that shirt's an ugly tent. You should pick up some benzoyl peroxide for your forehead—it'll clear those whiteheads right up."

I was speechless.

Realizing she hadn't primed me for that once-over, she smiled, sympathetic but not sorry. "You're beautiful Evie, you're just a mess right now. Don't worry—you'll figure it out." She shut the truck door and pulled out of the driveway.

I went to the MacQueens', let myself into the backyard through the rusted gate. Torq sat on a plastic lawn chair, sulking, petting one of his dogs. The MacQueens had at least three dogs at all times.

"Do you think I'm a mess?" I asked him.

"Do you think I'm shit?" he said.

I weighed the pros and cons of continuing this conversation. "I'll tell you if you tell me."

He thought about that. "Define mess?"

"Define shit?" I countered, childishly.

He glared. "Did I hit those notes?"

"I loved your song. Lugh'll love it too, as long as you don't tell him who it's about." I hoped that would be enough.

"But did I hit the notes?"

I gave it to him straight. "No."

He looked worried. "I want to sing my song. And I don't want to lose my voice."

I told him he should try the crazy Polish guy, but I knew he couldn't afford it. He was almost in tears, which made me uncomfortable and I would've walked away if I wasn't waiting for an answer to my question. But he had his answer, so he did the walking, slamming the storm door behind him, melodramatic as ever, leaving me to contemplate the meaning of mess while his dog pissed on my shoe.

After about fifty pages, you know me well enough to know I'm not that deep and didn't contemplate for long. I just needed some goddamned clothes, stat.

Dusty bellbottom jeans, tweed jackets, chain belts, wool blazer, combat boots, gogo boots, pinstripe button-downs, red and white striped ties, a fur-collared suede coat—the boxes were stuffed to the brim. No one would notice if a few pairs of old pants went missing.

"What're you doing?"

Lugh came back from watching Will play video games and caught me in his family's garage, my arms loaded down with clothes.

"I don't have any pants that fit."

"So you're stealing ours?"

"They don't fit you anymore," I mumbled, hugging the clothes to my chest. That wasn't his point. My parents made more money than his. He waited for a real explanation. All I could say was, "I look like a mess. I am a mess."

Lugh frowned. "Who told you that?"

"Isis."

"Isis is wrong."

"No she's Wong."

"I don't think you're a mess."

I rolled my eyes at him. "Yeah, but have you seen your room lately? I think we have different definitions."

"Why don't you go buy clothes? Our stuff is crap."

"I like your crap."

He looked at the clothes I'd picked. "You didn't take any of mom's stuff." It wasn't a question, or a judgment, just an observation.

"I like *your* crap," I repeated. The t-shirt on the top of the pile smelled of Old Spice deodorant, which Lugh MacQueen still wears.

Lugh helped me carry the clothes across the street. After Torq had calmed down, he brought me some old clothes he'd been hoarding in his closet. Torq drew a chart that showed all the possible outfit permutations I could get out of his charity while we all listened to some weird-ass Nordic faerie music Lugh's internet pen pal had sent him. (Five or six years later I'd rediscover the

HEIDEGGER STAIRWELL 53

band under the moniker Sigur Rós.) Then, because he thought it was a good idea, Torq pinned me on my stomach and cut my hair, reassuring me that "I wanted this," that "I'd like it." My mother, drawn to the ruckus in my bedroom, chased both boys out with a spritz bottle and took me to First Choice.

As we were driving there, she said, "Your clothes look very handsome, honey. Are they Torquil's?"

And I said, "Mom, I like wearing boy clothes."

She said, "Evie, do you remember that dress grandma bought you? The pink one with the satin bow and the crinoline. You were five or six. You cried when she put you in it, scratched her face, but she was going to get her picture of you wearing it. Do you remember what you did?"

I sighed.

"—She wanted you out on the porch. But it rained all night and there were big puddles everywhere. When you saw that puddle, you ran for it, jumped in the puddle, and rolled around in like a piglet until you were brown from head to toe—everything but the whites of your eyes and teeth. And you know? It was a much better picture."

First Choice cut my hair like Leonardo DiCaprio.

When I went home and chanced a look, I was stunned. The weird girl who lived in my mirror looked almost handsome. The blazer gave her broad shoulders, and the skinny pants highlighted her narrow hips, which suddenly looked right. I played with her hair until I got her bangs to fall just slightly in her eye. I almost didn't recognize her. And I almost did.

Monday morning Isis picked me up for school. "If I knew you'd get yourself together so quick I would've lectured you months ago." Isis stopped to let Lugh jump in the cab. "What does he think of your new look?"

> The magic of television. Her makeover took almost a month.—ISIS

"Why would Lugh care about what I wear?"

She shrugged. "I guess he wouldn't."

Will took one look at me and asked when I got a sex change. He was half serious. I had no comeback because I didn't know people could change their sex because my mother wouldn't tell me what a tranny was.

For three weeks after that, Torq didn't sing with the band. He was paranoid he was going to lose his voice and never sing again. So when he suddenly announced that he'd auditioned for, and won, the lead role in the school's production of *Show Boat*, the band felt cuckolded.

"Well, he did do three years of jazz and two of tap," was all Lugh said about it.

Torq tried to convince us he was trying to broaden his horizons as a singer, but no one was buying it. He hoped to distract us with the lyrics to a new song, but we were already plenty distracted. Off kilter, really. What would make an aspiring rock star sign up for a production of a seventy-year-old musical?

The band didn't have to wonder long; the answer stormed into the music room clutching the cast list in a white-knuckled hand, strawberry-blond hair bouncing with every purposeful step.

"Coco?" Isis stood. "What's wrong?"

Coco ignored her and stomped up to Torq, crumpled the cast list in one hand, and dropped it at his feet. "I'm not going to let you ruin my last high school musical, Torquil MacQueen."

"Hello dear. Nice to see you too." He picked up the paper, smoothing out the creases. "Gaylord Ravenal. Now that's the name of a confident man."

Coco said, "This may be a joke to you, but it's important to me. It's what I want to do with my life."

"And you should," said Torq, sincerely.

"What are you getting out of this?"

"Well, I hear we have a kissing scene." Torq leered.

"Ew. The whole school knows where you've been. I'm pretty sure I've contracted crabs just talking to you."

"Well then, if you already have them that makes things a whole lot easier..."

"Torq," Coco said, deflated, "what do you want?"

"I want to be a better singer," he said, sincerely. "You said this is hard stuff. *Real music*. I want to be able to sing it."

"You can't just will yourself to sing it. You need direction, training..."

"So I need help. Help me."

Coco shook her head and told him no. No. No. She left, less confident than when she came in.

And Torq smirked.

Will slammed his hands down on the piano. He never treated that piano well, using it as a TV tray, for his lunches, sitting on the lid, pushing it across the room whenever he felt like he had to prove his strength. "Tell me you did not join the school musical for some ginger pussy. There are easier redheads than Coco Coburn."

Lugh put up his guitar. "What's this about, Torq?"

"Isn't it obvious?" said Torq.

"To Will it is."

Torq rolled his eyes. "Singing lessons. Coco's going to teach me how to sing."

Lugh frowned. "She just said she wouldn't."

"That musical means too much for her to let a 'dilettante' like me ruin it for her. She'll come around."

Will asked me what the fuck a dilettante was. I didn't know so I rolled my eyes and called him an idiot.

"Just so we're clear, you are not trying to sleep with Coco, right?" said Isis. "Because she's my friend and I'm not comfortable with the drama I know that would cause." I got déjà vu.

Torq gave me a conspiratorial look. "Course not. I respect her as an artist. I think she can help us as a band."

Torq's descent into theatricality began a week earlier. We agreed to walk home together after our respective detentions. When we met, Torq gave me a new tie, saying it would go perfectly with the AC/DC outfit he'd given me the week before. He said my andro-schoolboy thing was working and told me I looked fuckable. He always said crap like that—no boundaries.

We heard music as we passed the gymnasium, and Torq

stopped and cracked the door for a peek. Unlike Torq, I'd heard Coco Coburn sing dozens of times before. She was my mother's favourite singer. Coco was the town diva, performing at ribbon-cutting ceremonies, drag races and fishing derbies. Contrarily, she was a mystery, antisocial, striding through the halls with snobbish certainty. As one of the few who knew her, it was obvious to me that she was overwhelmed, barely keeping her head above water after spending years treading it.

But Torq had never heard her sing. And to encounter it through Rachmaninoff's "Vocalise"... I felt his adam's apple bob against my temple.

When she was done, there was no applause, no bow, only the criticisms of an old Polish singer. She sang a line, and he made her sing it three more times, hating every instance more than the last. He got up on stage, put his hands on her jaw, her back, her abdomen. Torq bristled. She sang the line again, and he was satisfied. They did the same for another five or six sections of the piece.

"He's insane, she's perfect," Torq muttered.

"He's her teacher. That's what they do," I whispered. "That's how she became perfect."

They moved on to another piece. It was as if she'd created the playlist for Torquil just so he could be immersed in the ecstasy of the purified female voice. At the end of a *Rusalka* aria, I had to pull him away from the door so Coco's teacher didn't mow us down. He walked as purposefully as Coco—maybe she even learned her walk from him.

Coco came out a moment later. Torq, who was usually the one ensorcelling people, was spellbound. After watching Coco, he realized he was out of his depth.

"I was wondering who was spying on me. I should've told Dr. Rydz; he would've beaten your legs black and blue like they did in the old country."

Her sneer should've broken the illusion, but Torq was too far gone. He stared at her as though she were Mick Jagger or Paul McCartney. I was concerned.

"Your songs . . . were really nice."

Coco raised an eyebrow. "And?" she asked. She was looking for a punchline.

"And nothing."

Coco rolled her eyes at me, like we were girlfriends being bothered by some geek, clueless and socially stunted. In reality, Torq was popular and everyone thought Coco was a snob, which had some truth to it but it wasn't her fault. She was just clueless and socially stunted.

> It's not as if Evan was popular. It's just that whenever anyone bullied Evie, Torq and Will retaliated so most people left her alone. She was just as hated then as he is now. —COCO

"Move, Torq. I have another rehearsal to go to."

"What are you rehearsing?" He didn't move.

"Why?"

"Curious." They were close, physically. It's one of those things he does that either seduces people or creeps them the fuck out. Judging from Coco's curled lip and blush, it accomplished both.

"Auditions for next year's school musical are next week."

"School musical, eh?"

I should've seen the wheels turning then, but I was too worried he was going to kiss her or feel her up and that she would beat the shit out of him and I'd have to carry him home. Torq still often forgets his life partner has a black belt in karate. They have the English bodyguard for a reason.

Coco said, "What? You want to audition?"

"Maybe."

Coco pushed by him. If she noticed the way his hand drifted down her hip as she passed, she didn't acknowledge it.

"Even if you were serious, we're doing *Show Boat*. It's not a musical for dilettantes." She walked down the hall, a backlit silhouette. "By the way, you look nice today, Evie. I like your blazer."

Torq's eyes followed her until she was out of view.

"Torq. Don't."

"Don't what?"

"Fuck Coco. She's my friend." Sound familiar?

"Fuck . . . ?" He frowned. "You don't think much of me, do you?" He laughed. "I don't want to fuck her. I want her to teach me how to sing. And I know exactly how to make her do it."

I didn't like those words. No one made Columba Coburn do anything.

Torq worked his con with light hands, giving Coco space after the casting notice, both literally and figuratively, doing research so he could ask serious questions, about singing, about music. She dismissed him. But then his questions became more sophisticated: breath support, vowel placement in high notes, chest voice, head voice, mask, falsetto, vibrato, melisma. By the end of the second week she accepted that he wasn't making fun of her. By the end of the school year, they could be seen walking down the hall together. People talked, as they do in high school and anywhere fishbowlish. Torq MacQueen cannot be single! It is forbidden! But, oftentimes, Torq just wants to be alone.

I figured that was why he skipped his first prom to hang out with the rest of us losers in Will's basement, playing Sorry, eating Cheetos and sharing a six-pack of wine coolers my mother bought us to celebrate us passing our exams. I was winning. Casually I told them it was because I'd been playing Sorry with Coco every Monday night for the last eight years. Torq left to go to the washroom.

"Don't talk about her," warned Lugh. "Not tonight."

Torq came back and rolled his turn. Isis rolled and Sorryed Torq's game piece. He sighed. "I hate this game."

"Sorry," said Isis.

"Stop fucking saying that." He kicked the board and left.

Lugh put the board back together in vaguely the right configuration. "Told you."

"What's his damage?" Will downed his third wine cooler. There were five of us. "If he's so pissed, why doesn't he just go to the goddamn prom? I told him he can borrow my dad's tux."

"Your dad's like three hundred pounds," said Isis. "Torq and Evie could wear that like a donkey costume."

"Why aren't you at the prom? Isn't your girlfriend going?"

The only other lesbian we knew of in the school was a bulldyke on the wrestling team named Sheila. As far as I knew Isis

Libel: Sheila Frye is not a lesbian. She married a construction worker in Sudbury and has three kids.—**ISIS** and Sheila had never even talked. By accident Isis and I caught each others' eyes. She looked away quickly, blushing.

"Go talk to him, Evie," said Lugh.

Lugh usually treated me in a way that felt right, but he always assigned me as the sympathetic ear, which is ridiculous because I'm not that sympathetic. Not like him. "Why don't you talk to him?"

"Because I don't want to."

"I don't want to either," said Will.

"No one asked you. Go find him, Evie."

I chased Torq down. It wasn't hard; he was sitting on the front steps with a chocolate-chip cookie.

"Will's mom gave me this," he said with his mouth full.

"So what's going on? Did you have a fight with Coco? Is she not going to teach you?"

He kicked one of the quartz stones out of the garden, dribbling it between his blue Adidas. I kicked the rock away and flicked it back into the garden. "Torq?"

"She's gonna teach me. Twice a week."

So it wasn't Coco. "What's the problem?"

He shrugged. I still hate it when the MacQueens shrug. It speaks volumes without saying anything.

"Why didn't you go to the prom?"

He said he didn't want to, which was bullshit. The idea of prom sickened Isis, and Lugh hated crowds, but Torq ate that crap up. So I just said, "Why?"

He told me to fuck off. I'd known him too long to let him get away with that. When he tried to leave, I blocked him. He was bigger, but we both knew he'd never hurt me. After a short standoff, he sat his ass back on the stoop.

"I'm just tired of them."

I asked who.

"All of them. Everyone's just been up in my face lately. About nothing. In my business. I'm fucking exhausted."

I felt bad about literally getting up in his face.

"Coco didn't go to prom. She said if she went she'd end up

standing in the corner. She didn't think anyone would dance with her or even talk to her."

It sounded paranoid, but she was right. "That's an asshole thing for people to do."

"Right?" He shook his head. "They say mean stuff about her, Ev. I never noticed before."

Time for some honesty. "You make her stand out."

"So I'm an asshole for being her friend?"

"I didn't say that."

The porch light flickered.

"I want to leave." He said, suddenly.

"It's still early..."

"I mean Emmet Lake."

I heard it all the time at school, but never from Torq. "Where would you go?"

"Start over. The city. Find some anonymity. I fucked too much up here."

His life wasn't perfect, but it was pretty good. I couldn't think of anything he'd messed up himself. Not like me. My life was a shambles.

"She thinks of me like you think of me."

I assumed we were talking about Coco, but I didn't know what he meant. "Torq, I think you're one of the best guys I know."

"You think I'm a player. That I use people, that I get off on all the attention. I'm just superficial and a dilettante and..."

That didn't sound like me. I still didn't know what a dilettante was. "Torq, you know what Coco's like."

"She's amazing. And she's right. I'm a piece of shit."

I didn't know how to deal with him like this. We sat on the porch awhile, counting cars full of drunkards, trying to differentiate car horns from loon calls.

"Ev, I never wanted to nail Coco. I'm fucking in love with that girl."

By the end of the summer of 1997, Torquil MacQueen and Coco Coburn were together. They broke up the week before *Show*

Boat, got back together opening night, broke up at Christmas, got back together Boxing Day. Broke up at ... well, as of this writing, there has been one more breakup than reconciliation.

Between all of that, Torq became a singer. And through association, Heidegger Stairwell inherited Coco Coburn.

Miss Coburn came with an accessory, and his name was Pierre Clowes.

> This makes Pierre sound like a chihuahua. —**COCO**

Isis drove Lugh and me home that night. Torq walked. When she pulled into my driveway she turned off the ignition. Lugh jumped out of the cab. When I reached for my seatbelt, Isis kissed me. It didn't surprise me—we'd been dancing around this since the lake accident. I remember how gentle it was, but not hesitant. Her hair felt like feathers on my cheek. I opened my eyes only a second and saw Lugh standing at the driver's side door, staring at us.

Isis turned to him, lowered the window. "Gonna watch?"

Lugh stepped away from the truck, shaking his head. He wandered across the road and was nearly mowed down by a car speeding through the subdivision full of drunken idiots.

"His loss," said Isis. I wasn't sure I agreed. "You want to come to my house? My parents don't care what I do as long as it doesn't have a dick."

Isis and I lay together on her four-poster bed: me making fun of the drunken banter of the post-prom crowd on their zombie walk of shame, Isis running her hand over my neck, my arm, slipping it under my shirt (not finding much). Nervous, I told bad jokes and kept expecting her to shut me up, but she didn't. She kissed all my naked skin.

"I should stop talking, right? It's fucking incessant."

"You talk when you're nervous. I get it," she said. "How do I make you not nervous, Evie?"

I said I wasn't and kissed her to prove it to us both, but I was awkward, clumsy, raking my teeth against her lip. Our torsos barely connected.

"It's okay," she said. "We can take it slow. No pressure."

But there was pressure. I'd been thinking about this for months, building it up in my head. Being with Will, I'd known there was something wrong. It had to mean I was a lesbian. Doing this with Isis would let me know once and for all. I gathered my meagre wits about me and gave her a real kiss, wrapping my arms around her waist, pulling her roughly against my chest. My aggression surprised her, but she gave in, saying, "gentle, gentle."

> For the sake of the narrative, this section could use a few more details. —**TORQ**

Isis went down on me. And I cried.

> this is the least hot lesbian sex seen I ever pictured. —**WILL**

She sat up between my legs, ghost-white. It took me a moment to realize she had stopped. I'd been so far away, so removed from my body, I think I was astral projecting.

I pulled my shirt down, my pants up, sat cross-legged on her bed.

"Maybe we should go slow," I suggested, monotone. I was numb and cloud-headed.

Isis looked out the window.

"I'm distracted tonight. Maybe we could go back to kissing?"

"I'm not interested in experimenting with straight girls," she said. Her exhalation came out as a shudder.

"I'm not a..."

"You're not a lesbian, Evie," she said.

"You don't know that," I said, defensive.

Her laugh was sharp. "If you saw your face, you'd know it too. I don't know why you're trying to convince yourself you are." She strode to the window. The breeze caught in that long platinum hair, whipped it around her shoulders.

"There's something wrong with me, Isis," I said, quietly.

"No shit," she said, and then whispered, "You're such a fucking mess."

I didn't know which one of us she meant, but she would've been right either way.

> I don't know if that's exactly what we said, but the scene is accurate. I won't purport to know if it services the book, but don't take it out on my account. I'm not ashamed. I'll say Evie could stand to take out some of the racy details. It's a little smutty for a memoir. —**ISIS**

NOTE: I'm not sure I should keep this scene in. Let me know what Isis thinks. I don't want to piss her off. She barely talks to me as it is.

HEIDEGGER STAIRWELL 63

A Neverending Fire Drill

When Pierre was born, the ghosts of Bach, Mozart, Beethoven hovered above the delivery bed drinking wine while talking harmonic progressions, the function of virtuosity and about the self-indulgent whinging of the post-Beethovenian Romantics. They got sloshed and passed out before Pierre gathered enough nerve to leave his embryonic studio. Debussy and Stravinsky's ghosts snuck in, drew penises on the early masters' cheeks, and bestowed gifts of understatement, rhythmic experimentation and esotericism. Stravinsky left dodecaphonic earworms and Debussy, floating sound clouds Pierre has yet to expel from his work.

Wagner wandered by and left Pierre a gift as well: his famous sense of humour.

> Speaking of humour, sarcasm is the lowest form. Pierre deserves better.—ISIS

NOTE: Sorry, I don't know how to write about Pierre. I haven't forgotten what he said to me last time. As petty as I am, I can't write this and still maintain a modicum of professionalism.

I promise I'll write it later. Better yet, source out a ghostwriter.

Here: Pierre Clowes was an outsider everywhere he went. His father was a miner who left the family and Pierre was raised by his mother, the manager at the KFC. He was a sickly kid, like the hero of a nineteenth-century Russian novel. He began playing violin and piano when he was four, cello when he was six, and he composed his first song when he was eight. He was shy and honest, easily duped. Bullies singled him out, stole his lunch, threw him in trashcans, sat on top of him on the schoolbus.

Pierre's songs inspired me to be a better musician and person. But Torq and Evie were cruel to him. Torq felt threatened because Pierre knew so much more about music than he did, and Evie blindly backed Torq on everything. Torq has so many gifts—his life, besides what happened in Duluth, is charmed—so how he treated Pierre, who only really had one gift, was completely irrational. Somehow, despite all of that, Torq and Pierre had moments of intense creativity. Never together. Torq, intuitive, channelling some muse, pulled beautiful tunes out of the ether, scribbled them down on backs of receipts, napkins, math homework. And then Pierre would find them and turn them into masterpieces.

I don't know what Pierre said to Evan, but I'm sure he deserved it and has no right to be so indignant. He needs to be the bigger person.—**COCO**

A Dog Named Heidegger
DECEMBER 1998

A year or so before Y2K failed to destroy the world, my father took over my grandfather's company and my parents moved to Mississauga. I had six months left of school and I was eighteen, so I asked my mom if I could stay with the house in Emmet.

My mom: Evie, do you remember the treehouse your father built? You were so sure it was going to fall apart that you tried every way possible to prove yourself right—kicking the door, stamping on the floor, hammering the wall, sawing the rope ladder...

Me: I'm not going to demolish the house.

Mom: Your little Fisher-Price hammer was so cute. But that was a real saw.

My house became more than just a rehearsal space for... Unnamed Art Rock Outfit. When Torq tried to register Young Fogeys he found out that a group in Birmingham had already taken it.

So my house became more than just a rehearsal space for "the band" (but not The Band); it became a hotel. I was rarely alone, even at night—at least one of the band members was asleep in the house somewhere. Sometimes I'd wake up in the middle of the night and do rounds of the house to see who was there, listening for snoring at closed doors. Waking up had always been a strange time in my day. It was when I was reintroduced to my body, and it always felt like we were meeting for the first time. But that feeling faded walking those halls, hearing the sounds of people who had chosen to sleep in my house.

Torq would usually sleep in my parent's bed; Will slept in my father's La-Z-Boy, occasionally snoring, but always drooling; Isis didn't usually sleep over, but when she did it was behind closed doors, silently; Pierre didn't stay. And Lugh? He was practically permanent. He lived on the sofa in the den, the one I used to sit on to listen to my mother's lessons, where Coco and I played Sorry. Sometimes I'd watch for the blanket to rise and fall to make sure he was still alive. Ever since the incident at the lake, I'd had nightmares about Lugh dying, blind, his mouth full of blood. Every day when we sat for breakfast, I'd wave. He always waved back. I just wanted to make sure he could see me, even if it was obvious he could see enough to spoon Corn Pops into his mouth.

With no pretence of segue, I'm now going to go into how the Mac-Queens love animals. Relevancy will manifest in due time.

The MacQueens come from a family of animal lovers. Their father had lived on a farm in Caithness until moving to Canada. Mrs. MacQueen, the medievalist, had decorated their house with a slew of unicorn figurines. While the MacQueens could not manage cows, chickens, ducks, horses or unicorns, their home included three to five dogs, five fish, a snake, four well-stocked bird feeders, and a cat, to whom Lugh was allergic. Torq walked all three dogs for an hour every morning. Lazy ass couldn't get out of bed to shovel the driveway, but he'd cross glaciers with those slobbery monsters. Me, I can take or leave the menagerie. Kitten or puppy, sure. When they genetically modify them to never grow up, I'll take half a dozen, thanks.

An inch of snow on the ground. The band was rehearsing a new arrangement of "Freeman" when Lugh put down his guitar, eye trained on something out the window, and bolted. I had a flashback of Columba Coburn doing the same.

I ran to the window in time to see Lugh grab some rocks from the garden and start whipping them at a group of preteen punks across the street. They fled, and with the mob dispersed, everything was illuminated.

There was a dog. Its leg was caught in the neighbour's chain-link fence. It was panting and barking.

Torq ran across the street carrying a sheet of Bristol board. Torq loosely wrapped the Bristol board around the dog's head, like one of those cones, while Lugh untangled the its leg. When the dog was free, both backed away, slowly. The dog, some sort of rottweiler mix, licked at its paw and ran down the sidewalk. Satisfied, the MacQueens returned to the house.

"That dog could have bitten you," said Pierre as they walked in.

Torq glared. "No shit, that's why I brought the Bristol board."

"And you knew that was going to work, yes?"

"Stop nagging me Clowes—you sound like goddamn Coco."

Mention of Coco always shut Pierre up. It had been months since she'd left us for Toronto. Torq was supposed to go too, but stayed at the last moment, deferring university to work construction in Emmet and rehearse with the band. No one was surprised when they broke up, but no one knew whether the breakup precipitated Torq's stagnation, or vice versa.

Coco assured us she'd only broken up with Torq and not the band, but we hadn't heard from her since she left, and wouldn't until she and Torq got back together at Christmas. That still makes the band nervous.

[margin note: What the hell does this mean?—**COCO**]

They ran the song, Pierre and Torq squabbled over the bridge, they practiced it again. Pierre decided he needed to completely re-orchestrate the chorus, so they took a break. Isis baked pizzas, I put beer in the freezer to chill, Lugh played a classical song on his guitar and Will smoked on the front patio. A couple of minutes later, he stole an uncooked hotdog from the fridge.

After dinner, Will slipped out for another cigarette with two pieces of pizza. Isis muttered "Pig."

Torq said, "You know he's not eating that pizza, right?"

"What's he doing with it?"

"Dogs love pizza," said Lugh and played a guitar lick in D major.

Isis's eyes narrowed. "And wieners."

Torquil said, "Don't we all love our wieners?" He gave her shoulder a quick massage before joining Will outside, where we all eventually ended up.

On my parent's patio swing sat Will, smoking a joint in the middle of the day, and the dog, taking up two thirds of the swing, his head in Will's lap. The dog burped and it smelled of pizza, wieners and whatever else strays ate in the mean streets of Emmet Lake.

Torquil let the dog smell him. He got a lick. "Good boy, Heidegger."

"Heidegger?" Will choked on his smoke. "What the shit is that?"

"It's his name," said Torq.

"Who says?" said Will, indignant.

"His German heritage and philosophical mien."

And so the damn thing had a name.

"If you break that swing you have to buy Evie's parents another one," said Isis.

Will offered the joint, "Suck this, Sappho."

She passed it along to Pierre. "I don't do those things," he sputtered.

"Yeah, but you probably should," groused Torq.

This is not where I say that Torquil MacQueen was Pierre Clowes's gateway into cocaine, for which he is, at writing, getting treatment. This is where I say that Pierre Clowes was very private about his relationship with drugs and would claim to be a teetotaller for the next six months until he and Torq snorted coke off a stripper's sweaty tramp stamp at the biggest battle of the bands north of Toronto.

> Evie needs to change this.—**ISIS**

To calm himself after a long day of dealing with Pierre, Torq lit incense and took the lotus position. Since breaking up with Coco, he'd discovered Buddhism and was making a good show of it.

I asked Will if the dog had tags. He didn't even have a collar. I suggested calling animal control.

"No," said Lugh.

"Why not?"

"Because they'll gas him," said Lugh.

Torq opened his eyes, infuriatingly serene. "Look at Heidegger, Evie—do you want him to get gassed?"

Not knowing who Heidegger was, the irony of the statement was lost on me. "Then what do we do? We can't keep him."

"We call the no-kill shelter tomorrow morning," said Lugh.

I asked them what we do with him until then. It was a stupid question.

Like most nights, Lugh stayed. I'm sure he was afraid I would chase the dog off my property the moment he left, and his fears were valid.

I offered the backyard, which was fenced in with trees for the dog to piss on, and rain water to keep him alive. Lugh was afraid the damn thing would get cold, so in it came. It made itself right at home, sniffing all the soft surfaces, drinking from the toilet (joke was on him, it hadn't been cleaned in months), hoovering up the smorgasbord of floor crumbs that had accumulated since my parents left. I followed him around, terrified he'd lift his leg on my PlayStation, or Lugh's guitar, or anywhere, really, because I knew how to use the vacuum but I was pretty sure that didn't work for piss.

After the dog's grand tour, Lugh lured him into the den with bacon. He circled and flopped onto the shag. Lugh and I settled ourselves on the sofa to watch television. Our regular configuration was me sitting cross-legged at the head with him lying down, his pillow in my lap, his arm around my knee. When it was just the two of us, sometimes he took off his eyepatch, like he did that night. As he watched whatever bland sitcom was on television, I watched him, incapable of looking anywhere but his puckered, wrinkled eye socket, remembering all the ways he died in my dreams, and how he'd looked that night at the lake, his mouth full of blood, a shard of amber glass where his MacQueen-green eye had been.

Suddenly, instead of Lugh's face, a black-nosed, whiskered snout. Heidegger licked Lugh's face, his nose, his mouth, and began licking the damaged eye. The pink tongue flicked against

Lugh's pale skin, the red and white scars, the raised-relief ridges, the lashless lid, the prosthetic eyeball. Disgusted, Lugh laughed and pushed him away. The saliva smeared across Lugh's skin caught in the light of the television. He used his shirt sleeve to wipe it off. He wasn't gentle—he treated it like any other patch of skin.

Gingerly, with my heart in my throat, I touched my fingertips to his scar. I was surprised by how soft it was. I think I expected it to feel like plastic, but it was more the veins on a wilted leaf.

"Evie?"

I traced his eyeball, knowing the structure of the lids was formed by the prosthetic, the iris of which wasn't quite the right colour. Why the hell couldn't they have gotten the colour right? It wasn't as if the eye was doing anything else for him . . .

He looked up at me with his good eye, the iris of which was the colour of mint candies. "You okay?"

"Lugh, you're amazing."

"I know, right?"

"No, really."

"Psh." He watched the TV. A Mooseknuckle commercial flashed across the screen. To celebrate fifty years of rocking your taste buds, the company was sponsoring a battle of the bands. Winner received a recording contract. The host city was only a few hours away.

"You guys should do that," I said.

He shrugged.

I signed them up the next day.

I did the full rounds of the house that night. Even though the only person who fell asleep downstairs was Lugh when he was binge practicing, I checked it anyway. Two thirds of the way down the stairs, I stepped on something soft. I realized too late what it was. Heidegger yelped, bucked underfoot and sent me tumbling down the stairs. Lugh says I yelled and I must've because he turned on the light and came bounding up the stairs before I could right myself. Sure enough, there was the damn dog, lying on the fifth to last step. When he saw Lugh he thumped his tail. Lugh patted the dog—that dog that had almost ended me—as he stepped over him.

"What happened?" He checked me over. Nothing broken, everything bruised.

"Do dogs usually sleep on the stairs?" I asked the resident dog expert, trying to deflect the attention away from me.

"Not that I've seen." Lugh whistled. "C'mon, Heidegger."

Tail thump. Yawn. Nothing.

Lugh shrugged. "Guess he likes it there."

"Get rid of him or I will."

The dog wouldn't budge. Lugh, sleep deprived and a little stoned, seemed to think this was hilarious. I wasn't as impressed. "Get him out of my stairwell, Lugh MacQueen."

"I think it's his stairwell."

Lugh wanted me to go to the hospital but I assured him he was an idiot. I hadn't damaged my head—just my chin, which I treated with some disinfectant, and my ego, which I treated with self-deprecation. He followed me into my room and helped me into the bed. Then he sat down beside me.

"What're you doing?"

He fluffed his pillow—my pillow. "I will wake you up every hour to make sure you're not dead."

"I'm fine."

"Now. We'll see in two hours."

I didn't know what the big deal was. Will had fallen off our friend's boat last summer and hit his head on the hull. Lugh went in after him and pulled him up, like the goddamn hero he was, but he didn't sleep it off beside the lawn mower all night.

"How do you see me?" I said. Little precipitated the words—they just kind of appeared in my mouth.

He yawned. "What?"

I sat up, forgetting how sore my shoulder was until I used it. "What do you see when you look at me?"

He shrugged. "You."

"I'm serious."

"So am I."

So frustrating even then. "I mean, do you see me as, like, a girl? Or something else?"

"Is that what you want?"

"I want you to answer the question."

Lugh frowned. "What's going on with you?"

I didn't even know. "Forget it. Good night." I crawled under the blanket and turned away, regretting every word.

Lugh curled up beside me and whispered, "Sorry."

Poor Lugh. I lashed out and he apologized. But that's what he does—internalizes the suffering of the world, carries it like Atlas, even when it's a burden no one needs to bear. He's been on and off antidepressants for almost ten years, but they do little because it's not depression, but empathy.

To nip it in the bud, I turned over and kissed his eye socket. "You're my favourite person."

He smiled. "Wake me up in an hour so I can wake you up to make sure you're not dead."

Lugh woke me up after two hours. Satisfied, he let us both sleep the rest of the night.

But when I woke again, I couldn't breathe.

I opened my eyes; it was pitch. There was a suffocating pressure in my chest, and my yell came out as a gasp. All those medical TV shows flashed through my brain, and I decided I was having a heart attack due to blood poisoning from internal bleeding I'd suffered in the fall. At eighteen, I was going to die, because a dog decided to sleep in my stairwell. I hoped Torquil and Coco would sing at my funeral, and Lugh would find words for a eulogy. Isis needed to bake those peanut butter cheesecake brownies. I didn't want it to smell like my grandfather's funeral. I wish I'd kissed Lugh on the mouth instead of the eye.

"Heidegger, get!"

The pressure was gone and the air flooded back into my lungs. And I could see because there was no longer a big black dog ass on my face. The more air I gulped, the less I could breathe. Dizzy, I saw bright spots before my eyes. Above me, Lugh was looking around the white, characterless room like a madman. I kind of thought there were only two options for him: call an ambulance or hold my hand and watch me die, so I didn't know what the hell was going through his mind.

But it didn't matter, because he kissed me. And apparently he had a magic mouth, because before long, I could breathe again.

When he pulled away, I willed my lungs to stop working again. He sat up, looking sheepish. "I saw that on an anime."

Not a kiss. Rather, Lugh had used his mouth to regulate my breathing. I wasn't dying, just hyperventilating, and his mouth was no more magic than a paper bag.

He crawled off the bed and patted the dog sitting at the foot. "Let's get you outside before you kill Evie." As they left, I heard him say, "As of now, I think she preferred you as Heidegger de Stairwell."

Torq and Will showed up around ten to see Heidegger off. Lugh made him bacon. He gave me bacon too, and eggs, and toast, and a screwdriver, but he made the bacon for the dog. Bacon for the dog that had almost killed me. Twice.

The dog didn't give the shelter workers any trouble, wagging his tail when they put the collar on him. We said goodbye to Heidegger de Stairwell. We never saw him again.

Two weeks later, Lugh found out from a classmate who worked at the shelter that Heidegger had been destroyed.

Apparently, he had bitten one of the neighbourhood brats. Heidegger was deemed dangerous, given over to animal control and killed. Lugh had a meltdown and was sent home. He broke into my house and fell asleep on the couch with his guitar. Torq and I found him there.

"I think we should name the band after Heidegger. The dog, not the Nazi. In his memory," said Lugh.

"Okay," said Torq, without protest.

"Heidegger of the Stairwell. No—just Heidegger Stairwell."

> this chaptr is suposed to be about the dog so why is there all that gayness in it?—**WILL**

O Brother

For those who don't know, Mooseknuckle is a cheap lager brewed in Thunder Bay. It has a bubbly golden colour with an inch-thick white head that takes about ten minutes to shrink to a three-quarter inch lace. Highly carbonated, a chalky mouth-feel, both bitter and saccharine and faintly tasting of moose piss, it is the beer of choice when you are northern, sixteen and driving a snowmobile through the bush, half in the bag.

Fact: It's Will's favourite beer.—**ISIS**

This was reflected in the rock outfits that signed up for the Battle of the Bands in Sudbury. In fact, I think there was a band called The Snowmobilers, and I know there was one called Half-in-the-Bag, because we played them in the semi-finals and they weren't terrible.

This was February 1999. Coco came back from university so she could perform with us. We left at seven a.m. to get there for registration. Like now, the band doesn't do mornings. Torq backed us into a snowbank as he was pulling his parent's cleaning van out of the driveway. Will called shotgun, so Pierre, who gets motion sick, blew chunks in Coco's hair somewhere around Massey. Pierre would've aimed for me if he wasn't too busy looking down Coco's shirt. Lugh played the guitar the whole way, Isis listened to Bach on her Discman, and Will slept it all off.

Torq had three espressos. Aloud he wondered what the arena was like, if they'd leave the Canadian and American flags up, how many spotlights there were, if they had scrims, what the sound equipment was like, if they had headset mics—Lugh, for fuck's sake play something cheerful!—how many bands there would be, how many good bands there would be, how many country bands there would be, how many bands would be wearing plaid, if Heidegger should have worn plaid—Goddamn it Pierre!—what was Coco going to wear now?, if other bands had girls, if other bands had girl drummers which was hot, or girl guitarists, which was also hot, he wondered aloud if Coco would go down on him in the bathroom because he was getting hot thinking about girl drummers and girl guitarists, why was Coco being such a prude, why was Coco mad at him? . . . Will woke up just to turn the stereo on.

Scraggly beards were hip that year, as was greasy shoulder-length hair and chain belts. But that was so 1997 for Heidegger Stairwell. Torq stood in line wearing tight eighties-style black jeans, a corduroy jacket with one elbow patch, Lisa Loeb glasses with no lenses and a dirty-ole t-shirt upon which he'd scribbled an Anarchy sign in red marker, and on which Lugh had written in his little boy handwriting: "tavism." Will wore silver Nike track pants, a button-down shirt and a backwards cap; Pierre sported his father's pinstripe suit and a green tie; Isis a canary yellow bikini top, hip hugger jeans and a henna tattoo of a lily around her exposed belly button; Lugh, jeans, a The Band t-shirt, his black and white maple-leaf eyepatch and a weird Kabbalah pendant; finally, Coco wore a flowery skirt and my plain black t-shirt, which she stretched with her womanly attributes. Under my coat I was now wearing Mr. MacQueen's white button-down, which he kept in the car in case he had to clean fancy houses.

A blond girl in a Canadian tuxedo sidled up and asked if I was a reporter. I grunted "yeah"—why the hell not? She asked me if I was Shawn O'Somethingorother from the *Sudbury Illiterate Times* and, without waiting for my answer, told me her name and that she was the one who emailed me on behalf of her band, The Ruby Slippers. She knew I was young, but not sooo young! But of course I was—I was the only cool journalist at the *Sudbury*

We-Only-Edit-Captions Rag. Here, she needed to introduce me to the rest of the band—I was totally gonna to love 'em.

She slipped her arm through mine and led me into the arena. This was my chance to scope out the competition. Looking back, I caught sight of Lugh, standing behind his brother as Torq paid the entry fee. I believe I grinned at him.

The Ruby Slippers were an all-girl group, but not like the Spice Girls because Ruby were rockers who played their own instruments and wrote their own songs and didn't have gimmicky names or go around spouting insipid slogans, said the red-haired front woman with the nose ring and the striped knee socks. I took out the little tape recorder I always brought to gigs, and asked about their songwriting process, how they got together and how they felt about Riot Grrrl, or standing on the shoulders of bands like The Gogos or The Bangles. The singer sneered and asked me if that was the band who wrote that stupid Egyptian song.

They played. Faddish and ignorant yes, but also hot. The singer had this Shirley Manson thing going on. The guitarist put power in those chords—the antithesis of Lugh, for whom everything always looks so effortless. As they rehearsed, I fought a battle with my nagging doubt about the odds of Heidegger winning against Ruby Slippers. Heidegger Stairwell were better musicians, but incongruous in this flannel power-trio landscape. My thoughts were of subterfuge, and I considered the ways I could destroy this posse of maladjusted bitches so my misfits could win. Machine heads, tension rods and their partner lugs, the lead singer's water bottle—a half dozen ways to sabotage the band came to mind.

And Ruby Slippers could be the worst of twenty bands. I needed to be Shawn O'Somethingorother a little longer. I checked myself into the bathroom to ensure I looked professional—fixed the collar of the oversize shirt, smoothed down my cowlick. It was only then that I realized I also had to look like a man. It hadn't registered that the blond girl had not only mistaken me for Shawn O'Somethingorother, she'd mistaken me for a guy. When I was younger, it was exciting when people thought I was a son, a neighbour boy, some pervert going into the woman's change room. This time, no reaction; it was just a given. If I hadn't been on a mission to destroy all the garage bands in Northern Ontario, it would've perplexed me.

I visited every band. Most were auditory diarrhoea with meaningless lyrics, strings of uninspired bar chords and band names that made less sense than Heidegger Stairwell, which is already nonsense. But there were a couple besides Ruby Slippers that had potential.

Finished with my danger assessment, I joined Heidegger in the dressing room. The ever-present scent of old sweat, jock straps and pine-fresh deodorant reminded me of dating Will Sacco. Pierre sat at the far end of the wood-slot bench and Will played paradiddles on the wall. I hunkered down beside One-Eyed Lugh as he tuned his guitar.

"Where is everyone?" I asked him.

Lugh shrugged. "Who was that blonde?"

"Guitarist for a girl group. Don't tell Torq: he'll cream himself."

Lugh said, "Do you know her?"

"To her I was some reporter."

"So you played along?"

I gave him a look, which nurturing Lugh MacQueen would've roughly translated as "of course I did because I'm incapable of questioning or controlling my own behaviour in my constant pursuit of amusement" even though what I'd meant to communicate was "of course I did, jackass."

A voice cut through the crowd, a laugh like a crystal windchime. Coco pushed mere mortals out of her way to return to Heidegger's corner of the room. Her face was flushed, radiant, her pupils dilated. Pierre blushed. Torq followed and he had the same look, but smugger. It wouldn't have mattered if every other band was all-girl, not at that moment. Wouldn't matter to Pierre either.

> What does that mean?—**COCO**

First Round. Heidegger Stairwell vs. Pop-punk-plaid band No.1.

I sat in the stands, between a goateed guy and a couple of

burnouts, watching the show through puck-dented Plexiglas. Heidegger's opponents were a three-piece with a tone-deaf singer and a power-chord guitarist. Their drummer was far too sophisticated for the band, pounding out syncopations, ironically robotic flanges, oh, and a sudden 7/8 bar no one would ever think to play against a guitar in 4/4 time. Fuck, that dude was brilliant. I gave them a standing ovation. As soon as they were gone, Heidegger marched across the cement floor with their instruments, strange and flamboyant, NorOntario's version of Pride. All my snark vanished, and I sat, rubbing my suddenly cold hands.

> Musicians may get that Evan's being ironic here, but most readers probably won't. Or drummers.—**ISIS**
>
> that guy wasnt that hot—**WILL**

The guy with the goatee took a few photos as the band set up. His camera looked expensive and he had five or six lenses in his carrying case, in addition to a couple of Moleskine notebooks, a collection of ballpoint pens and a cell phone smaller than any I'd ever seen.

This was Shawn O'Somethingorother. My nervousness was exponential.

Lugh did some fine tuning on his guitar while Will arranged his kit to his precise specifications. Torq wandered, humming, and Coco taped down a few stray electrical cords so he didn't trip, which fans have seen him do many times when he and Coco were estranged. Isis was pale, cracking her knuckles, staring at her keyboard. Pierre plugged in his electric cello and arranged the pick up on the violin. He was vibrating with anticipation.

Smash crash rattle—Will dropped a cymbal. Isis's face went green. She turned quickly, leaned over the edge of the stage and threw up. I had palpitations and wondered if I was having a heart attack, which gave me more palpitations.

Isis returned to her instrument with all the grace she could afford. Will fixed his set.

Torq took his place in front between Pierre and Coco, who had a bass guitar hanging from her shoulders. Lugh joined Coco at her mic. Coco glanced at Torq, who gave her a wink. They launched into the opening of "Freeman Shuffle," those four bars of drunken, dissonant Beach Boys-esque harmony with a violin descant. That snarling guitar slide, the quirky bass line and the hiccupping beat.

By the end, the beat and the bass hook won over the crowd. As Torq let the last note fly people were on their feet. Not the stoners beside me (apparently they couldn't feel their feet and thought they had lost them), or Shawn O'Somethingorother, but people stood. O'Somethingorother made notes in his Moleskine.

Closing he book, he looked at me. "What'd you think of that... what's your name, kid?"

"Ee . . . " I was suddenly hyperaware of the last few hours, of the blond girl's lingering body spray on my sleeve, of the way the collar of the shirt settled around my neck, of how I sat, how my legs felt, how big my feet looked in Torq's old Docs, and I said, "-van."

"*Even?*"

"Evan." I corrected. "Evan Strocker."

He accepted that. "Evan Strocker, what do you think about... what's this band's name?" He checked the flyer. "Heidegger Stairwell. Christ, that's stupid. So what do you think about Heidegger Stairwell?"

What a loaded question.

My mind whirled with possibilities, hundreds of hoity toity things to say to impress this reporter, to coerce him into loving Heidegger. But I decided on: "Those are some fucking amazing musicians."

He looked around the arena. "These people have no idea what they just heard."

"And what did we hear?"

"The future." He laughed. "I don't know if this place is ready for it, but they're getting it."

The judges advanced Heidegger Stairwell to the second round, where they would face off against a band from Huntsville who thought they were Great Big Sea. The band wasn't great, but they were in tune and had fun playing together. And they were accessible—unlike Heidegger in those days.

The Ruby Slippers were in the next heat. They pumped the crowd. Compared to Heidegger, they were the hometown underdogs in bitch boots and sneers. Their lyrics were platitudes linked like sausages, but it didn't matter what they said, only how they said it.

"Evan Strocker," said Shawn O'Somethingorother, "what did you think about Ruby?"

My first inclination was to badmouth them to build up Heidegger. I didn't do that. "They have a cohesive sound. They have that whole Runaways thing going. They're powerful women, or at least style themselves as such. Technically they're lacking, but with some coaching..."

"I agree," he said. "And they're very Now."

That was what I was afraid of.

Heidegger won the next round against Lacking Small Pond. The competition broke for dinner. Shawn told me he was going to interview Ruby Slippers, but I told him I saw them leave already and suggested he interview Heidegger Stairwell. I liked the guy—he liked my band—and didn't want it to end so quickly, which it would once Ruby told him they'd already been interviewed by another Shawn who matched my description. While O'Somethingorother was in the john I found Torq and told him to invite the reporter for dinner. I also told him to refrain from talking about me, which I knew the band did when I wasn't there.

And me? I invited myself out to dinner with The Ruby Slippers. We went to a local diner and talked about them. The blond guitarist had her hand on my thigh most of the night and it drifted up at imperceptible increments until she was an inch away from my anti-bulge. The conversation eventually drifted to Heidegger Stairwell.

"I do not understand that band at all," said the blonde. "Are they alternative? Are they rock? Are they, like, retro? Why do they have so many instruments? Why is there a violin? They look like they shop at the dump."

The singer lit a cigarette. "Maybe, but I'd trade you for their guitarist, though. Every time he has a solo I imagine those long fingers playing in my cunt."

Bitch.

Blond Guitarist: "Ew. He's dressed like a pirate."

Round Three: Heidegger Stairwell vs. Half-in-the-Bag

Half-in-the-Bag was an inappropriately named pop-rock outfit that hung around in minor keys and had a soulful, tortured lead singer, like an atheistic Creed. While Heidegger warmed up, I visited the competition as they set up the stage. I had just planned to kill some time But I saw the transpose button on the keyboard, and a black permanent marker one of the organizers had left on the stage. Half hidden behind amps, no one saw me change the tuning of the keyboard, or colour in the warning light. No one noticed me leave either, swiping their electric tuner and tossing the marker in the garbage.

Shawn O'Somethingorother told me how impressive the "Heidegger Kids" were. I wanted to yell, "Hell yeah! That's my motherfucking band!" Instead, I said I was looking forward to their next performance.

Half-in-the-Bag stepped up to their instruments.

A power ballad. A soaring melody rife with emotionalism, underpinned with intense minor-major transitions in the guitar and heavy toms. All of which were out of key. Shawn O'Somethingorother made a face. The band didn't hear it at first—the amps were in front and they couldn't hear themselves blended, only separate. The guitarist noticed in the chorus, but he kept playing, finding breaks here and there to try to adjust his tuning. He thought it was him. The singer thought he was off too and tried to compensate, some notes adjusting to the keyboardist's key, some to the guitarist.

> He never told me about this so I'm not convinced it actually happened . . . —**TORQ**

It was so excruciating, it was ecstasy.

Judge me all you will, but who's the bigger jerk—the asshole who did it, or the asshole who's living vicariously through said asshole by reading about it?

> Fact: Evie is. I hope that band sues her.—**ISIS**

Heidegger Stairwell sounded more amazing than usual in comparison. They advanced to the finale to play against The Ruby Slippers.

We stayed at a motel that night, all seven of us crammed into one motel room with two double beds. Coco and Isis shared a bed and Pierre slept at the bottom of it. Will said it was too gay to share a bed with dudes so he slept in the chair with his feet on the console table. Torq, Lugh and I shared the other bed.

When everyone was asleep, and my mind was just starting to fuzz, Lugh whispered to me, "I know what you did."

The Finale: The Ruby Slippers vs. Heidegger Stairwell.

I fantasized all morning about how to sabotage Ruby Slippers. Half-in-the-Bag had fallen right in my lap—I knew it wouldn't happen twice. While Heidegger warmed up in the dressing room, I paid the girl band a visit.

Blond Guitarist was in the hallway tuning up her guitar. I let her chatter at me. Eventually I pretended to get lethargic, sleepy, yawning. She became self conscious, asked me if she was talking too much. I didn't deny it, said I could use a coffee. The eager beaver told me she'd fetch me one and I let her, knowing the line was out the door at the canteen.

Blond Guitarist was rough with her instrument. She'd reconsider her poor technique after this performance. I twisted the low e-string machinehead until it was lax, then pulled out the metal nail clipper I'd stolen from Coco that morning. I found the most eroded point on the string and went at it, bending it, snipping at it to weaken it just enough. Then I tuned the string back up and did the same to the A and D strings.

She came back with my coffee and lightly strummed as I sipped.

The stage was decked out for the finale: extra spotlights, a ceiling-high screen backing the stage, complete with digital lightshow (all sweet for 1999). The Mooseknuckle people opened up the rink for a mosh pit, and the arena verged on crowded. Everything was dark but the stage and the red carpet runner leading to it.

I was giddy watching The Ruby Slippers step into the stadium. Musicianship would triumph over industry today, and I was its unsung hero. Evan—that was my superhero name, and like Superman, it was my true identity.

Last out was Blond Guitarist. She was carrying Lugh's spare guitar.

I found Lugh in the hallway, watching Ruby Slippers take the stage. Seeing me, he turned and walked into the Ruby dressing room. I followed him in.

"Are you fucking kidding me?" I snapped. My blood pounded in my ears and I could feel it in my neck. "You've ruined everything! Damn you Lugh MacQueen. Damn it!" I yelled, kicked the drum case against the wall.

Lugh grabbed my shoulders. I snarled at him to let me go. I hated his face and his stupid pirate eyepatch. He tightened his grip. "Do you really think they're going to win?"

"You're hurting me."

He didn't relent. "Do you think they're better than us?"

"Of course not. They're lame and derivative and they can't play worth shit."

"Then why did you do it?" he said, infuriatingly patient.

"Do what?" I said, mocking him with innocence.

"You know."

My resolve was failing. I was afraid I was going to cry. "Lugh, stop."

"What happened to your faith in us?"

"It never went anywhere. I just couldn't . . ."

"Couldn't what?"

"Leave it to chance!" I gasped. "You are the only fucking thing I believe in in this entire world. But I don't believe in this goddamn joke of an industry. And those bitches don't even deserve to share a stage with you. You deserve this! You are perfect." I stopped, realizing I was no longer talking about the band. His hold on my arms went slack and I hugged him, burying my head in his shirt so he didn't see my shame.

Lugh was patient. It's not like it was the first time I'd ever spazzed on him.

"Things happen how they're supposed to happen. We can't control everything. You know that."

"No I don't," I said, childishly.

He chuckled and I felt his abdomen ripple against mine. A shiver went up my spine.

"We're going to play the best we can," he said. "If we don't win we don't win."

"And then I set the place on fire," I grumbled, which was the solution I always offered.

"The band knows you how much you love them. We love you too, Evie."

And that was the moment I needed. "Evan."

"What?"

"I think I want you to call me Evan."

He paused. "You think?"

"I know."

It felt like years before he said, "Okay."

I was so light it seemed as though the only force anchoring me to the ground was the weight of Lugh's arms on my shoulders. And I clung to him so I didn't float away, because I didn't want to miss a second of the incredible life he would have.

Will stood in the doorway wearing his "duh" face. "Yo, we're running the song, get your ass back." He left and then came back. "And don't make out with Evie when she's dressed like that. You look like a homo."

"Evan," corrected Lugh. Another "duh" face, so Lugh explained. "Evie wants us to call her Evan now."

Will didn't understand. He just said, "Dude, we have like ten minutes before we go on—who cares? I'll call her Frankenstein if it'll get your ass in gear." He left.

Lugh stopped at the door. "You coming ... Ev?"

"I'll be there in a sec."

I watched him leave.

Her.

I didn't correct them. Changing my name was already a lot to put on them; it'd be too much to ask them to change their pronouns, especially with a concert to play and a battle to win. But

HEIDEGGER STAIRWELL 85

that was when I knew who I was. I was someone who would do anything for the people I loved, even if it ruined me. And I was a man.

Their first green room was a hockey dressing room, with cement block walls and wooden benches, as if the country was saying: "Remember this when you get famous. You belong to us."

They waited. Coco hummed to keep her voice warm. Torq sat on the bench and downed a bottle of tepid lemon water. Isis, all puked out, touched up her makeup. Will and Lugh were playing some punching game. Pierre paced, cracking his neck. I leaned against the wall beside Torq.

"Look at you," I said. "You've made it."

"We're on our way." His eyes drifted over his motley crew. Suddenly, he jumped to his feet, nearly colliding with Pierre. "There is a serious lack of energy in here." Torq shook Pierre and I think I heard the violinist's teeth rattle. "C'mon! This isn't a competition any more—this is a fucking rock concert! There's almost a thousand people out there!" (Just over six hundred.) "And they're here to listen to us. Smile a little—we've wanted this our entire fucking lives!"

Lugh smiled a little, as ordered. "Well, *you* certainly have."

Torq gave him that. "Unabashed. But Pierre here wants it too." Torq laid his palm on Pierre's chest. "I can feel the energy pulsing. He is shaking with anticipation."

"He's shaking because you're feeling him up and he likes it," said Will.

Torq grabbed Will's sticks out of his hand. Will chased him. Torq held them over his head and when Will reached for them, Torq hit him with one of the sticks.

"C'mon you lazy fuck. Stop sleeping off life." He played a drum roll on Will's forehead until Will snagged the sticks and began whipping Torq with them. Torq grabbed Isis off the bench and pulled her into a waltz, pitting her between himself and Will. Will knew better than to hit Isis, so he backed off, bided his time while Torq spun Isis around the room, cackling like a loon. She yelled at him to stop or she would spew. He dipped her dramatically and stole a kiss.

"You really want me to throw up in your mouth, don't you?"

Torq released Isis and grabbed Coco. He leaned in to kiss her. She closed her eyes, puckered her lips. Torq ducked and lifted her onto his shoulder in a fireman's carry, spanking her as she screamed. She escaped, then attacked him, red-faced and breathless. He tripped over Lugh's guitar case and fell to the floor laughing soundlessly, tears beading in the corners of his eyes.

Lugh picked up his brother. Torq wrapped him in a bear hug.

"Heart on your sleeve," said Lugh.

"Play yours out," finished Torq, thumping him on the back. He motioned everyone over. No one moved.

I pushed off from the wall. "We're in a locker room. He wants to huddle."

"That's football," said Will. "And huddle my ass; he's a MacQueen, he wants a group hug."

"Then we cuddle." I slid an arm around each MacQueen.

Torq gave me a loud, ferocious kiss on the temple.

"It's okay, I don't need to be pumped up," I said.

"You're amused."

I told him "mildly," as he was acting like a mental patient.

"No. You're. A. Muse."

The band hugged it out. The production assistant knocked on the door.

When the light rose on Heidegger Stairwell, when the plaintive two-tone wail of "O Brother" rang out, when Will put his rage into the tribal tom toms and Pierre his unrequited love into the bow of the cello; when Isis hit the lowest A on the keyboard, and Coco, six As above that; when Torq spoke for all of us, and Lugh, the only way he could, I sat in the dark of that stadium and sobbed, with joy, with shame, with relief, protected by the music. By the end of "One-Eyed Lugh" I was dry and I stood with the rest of the crowd, roaring louder than anyone, clamouring for more.

The Ruby Slippers won.

Two judges to one.

Heidegger Stairwell stood on the sidelines and watched the women collect their novelty cheque. They were all class, clapping graciously for the winners.

I was furious, and so were others in the audience. Some booed; I quietly seethed.

After the photos, both bands were whisked away to the after party. As he left the arena, Torq looked up at me. Epitome of optimism, he yelled, "We're on our way!"

They left me stranded when the house lights came up.

"That was unexpected," said Shawn, collecting his equipment. "I'm curious to know what the judges were thinking."

"They weren't," I said, petulant.

He buttoned up his coat. "Going to the party, Evan?"

"Why would I?"

"I was told you're Heidegger Stairwell's manager."

My cheeks were hot. "Who said that?"

"Heidegger Stairwell. The guitarist was very apologetic. He said you used my identity to spy on the other bands."

The jig was up. "So what if I did?"

He laughed. "You got balls, kid."

I really must've. "Actually, I don't."

It took him a second, but he was smart and knew more about the world than I did. "No shit?" He offered me a ride to the party.

We got to the bar late because I gave Shawn O'Something-orother a blowjob in the parking lot. (FYI, I do remember Shawn's last name but I doubt he'd want me to use it since he's some big shot at the *Globe and Mail* or *Star* or something.)

The bar was packed and no one was carding. Shawn handed me a glass. I washed my mouth out with whisky and spat into a garbage can. His spunk tasted like broccoli and lemons. I hung out by the bar and someone else bought me a drink—rather, he bought himself a drink but when he turned to chat up some hired girl I swiped it.

By the bathroom, I saw three men in business suits lead Torq into one of the side rooms. They closed the door, but the latch didn't snag. I took that as an invitation and snuck in, settled behind the partition wall separating the lounge from the entry.

I still have a recording of the ensuing conversation, but for legal reasons I can't print a transcription. So here's the gist:

(Scene: In the speakeasy. THREE MEN IN BUSINESS SUITS AND FEDORAS sit on a sofa. Across from them in a club chair sits TORQUIL MACQUEEN.)

INDUSTRY SUITS: Look, we think you're aces, kid. A real live-wire. And we wanna offer you the deal of a lifetime. We're putting together a singing act, see? Five good-looking Joes, right fellas, the kind the dames go nuts over. You: right up in front, making the kittens purr. With your pipes and our connections, you'll be raking in the dough.
TORQ: But my band . . .
INDUSTRY SUITS: Your band's swell, kid, but that sort of jazz ain't for most cats. It's a crummy biz—hotsy totsy players ain't worth a plugged nickel in this racket. You're lucky we rigged the game. You're free, kid—toss the dead weight.

> This never happened—Torq would've bragged about it. And why are they speaking like a Jimmy Stewart movie?—**COCO**

> wtf? the batle of the bands was rigged?—**WILL**

> This feels strangely accurate.—**TORQ**

I waited for Torq by the door. When he walked out, I grabbed him by the collar and pulled him into the men's washroom. He pushed me off.

"What's that in your hand?" I demanded. I knew what it was: their crummy contract.

He flipped through the pages. "I don't know."

I told him I heard everything; he said he could tell from the way I stretched out his t-shirt. I asked him what he was going to do. Torq flipped to the end of the contract. "I'm just going to look at it for a bit."

It was tempting; the cheque was right there, had his name on it and everything.

"This would really help my parents," he said. "And Lugh could go to university."

"Lugh would rather play music with you."

He sighed. "What they said about Heidegger..."

"They would say anything to get you," I said. "Because they're wrong about Heidegger, but they're not wrong about you."

He smiled, bashful. "I'm nothing special. I'm just surrounded by special."

"No," I corrected. "That's me."

Torq thanked the suits, but told them he hadn't worked his ass off creating a band he could be proud of, writing songs he loved about things he understood, only to have his chances sabotaged by number jockeys who wanted him for their doll set of auto-tuned metrosexuals in matching dinner wear.

"Don't tell the band," he told me over whisky.

"Why not?" The idea of Torq in a boy band was great teasing fodder.

"Because I don't want them to know why we didn't win. It'll be a shitstorm." He spied Coco approaching us. "We're gonna make it. I know it." Even after all that, Torq was still hopeful.

"How do you know that?" I said.

He showed me his canines. "We're going to be the biggest fucking band in the world, or I'll kill us trying." He finished his drink and turned around to stick his tongue in Coco's mouth. She berated him for disappearing. She told him Pierre needed cheering up and since Torq looked cheery, it was his job.

After that, the rest of the night was a blur. Torq found Pierre in a back room with a baggie of cocaine he'd "stumbled on." Pierre told Torq he didn't know what it was or what to do with it. All Torq knew was if you gave a girl a bump she'd probably let you do one off her stomach or between her tits, so he found them a hired girl. Coco, stone cold sober, stumbled in on them, with piss-drunk Pierre snorting a pinch off a stripper's oiled-up ass. She and Isis took the Greyhound home. Will slept with a forty-year-old who turned out to be the DJ's mistress and he got in an "altercation" with one of the DJ's entourage. And Lugh talked to a girl.

Ruby's lead laughed, touched her collarbone, gave him privileged views of her cleavage. Lugh smiled shyly, obviously enjoying the attention. When I saw them together, all I could imagine was them on top of the bar, his fingers in her. On our way home I made sure to tell him about her chlamydia.

Three days later, my doorbell rang at eight a.m. Lugh reached the door first. He stood there, his black and white pyjama bottoms perched precariously on the subtle curve of his skinny ass, eye naked for the world to see. I could hear Will snoozing in the bedroom.
"Did we get a package?" I yawned.
He frowned. "It's the people from Mooseknuckle."
His hands were empty. "Where's the package."
"No package. They're on the porch and want to come in."

The day after the competition I had Purolated the recording of Torq getting gangbanged by those industry assholes and I threatened to hand the story over to Shawn O'Somethingorother unless the band was compensated. Mooseknuckle announced that, due to fan support, Heidegger Stairwell would be given ten thousand dollars to record an EP and tour the Canadian heartland that summer. I sent a copy of the recording to the label as well, just to be a dick.

Trans-Can Flat

The *Freeman Shuffle* EP included six songs. The title track is a Beach Boys inspired upbeat tune with a crunch I'd see in early Franz Ferdinand; "Bad Moon" a narrative vocal showcase that sounds like the love child of David Bowie and Sonic Youth; "O Brother" is musically low-key, piano-based, with clever lyrics, a catchy guitar hook and a band sing-a-long; "Neverending Fire Drill" is a hard rock anthem fighting with a siren-like string arrangement; "Hope Is in a French Hospital" is a bitter sweet bilingual duet sung by a French man and an English woman influenced by Neutral Milk Hotel and Tori Amos; and then "One-Eyed Lugh," the most obvious precursor to Heidegger's later work, a huge emotional soundscape with bombastic percussion and ecstatic virtuosity strategically undermined with understated lyrics and quirk harmonies.

The EP has multiple personalities, like many first albums, but all contained in the same body. It's still from an era when the construction of an album meant something, unlike so many released in this iTunes age. When you listen to the album, you can see the shift, the body taking on the next personality, the features moulding to new specifications. It's juvenile in that sense, uncertain of its own identity, and experimental like a college freshman. It's not sonically perfect—but it's pretty goddamn close for me. Me and my objectivity.

A couple of years ago I was having a wet lunch in the Bowery with a certain New York writer who will remain anonymous because he's a douchebag and I don't want to give him any free publicity. But he's that guy, you know, the one who wrote that gimmicky novel about the angsty thirty-year-old lit-school-educated straight white man who has so many problems, like unrequited love and feeling adrift in a cruel world. But anyway, after I interviewed him for *Spin*, he deigned to ask me about myself, more specifically, about Heidegger Stairwell because he was a fan of *In from the Cold*, which he'd seen performed live. Was there a moment that defined Heidegger Stairwell for me, that encapsulated my experience with them? I told him about the time Heidegger Stairwell won the Battle of the Bands because I sabotaged their competition and the band thanked me for always believing that their talent would ensure their success.

> Fact: This is false. Evan and "anonymous" are still very good friends. I don't know why he would say this.—**ISIS**

> Replace "novel" with "memoir" and "straight" with "trans" and you basically describe this book. I can't tell if Evan's clueless or being ironic.—**TORQ**

He was a novelist—I thought he'd appreciate some fiction sprinkled in. Just a small amount—in the details, D'Agata-size, not Frey.

> Evan's attempt to seem literate. He's never read either of those books.—**TORQ**

But as I polished off my bottle of wine, I thought about what that moment was for me. It's taken me some time to figure it out, and here it is: me standing on the side of the Trans-Canada highway along the coast of Lake Superior beside a broken-down cube van with a flat tire, Lugh MacQueen sitting at my feet, blinded by an ancient beer bottle and a recent punch to the good eye, Torq MacQueen thumbing down a delivery truck to chase Coco Coburn who'd thumbed a ride only seconds before. No one else is here because someone stole a van, someone is injured, and someone hijacked a Greyhound bus. I am stoned after smoking up to calm the irregular heartbeat I've developed from starting a steroid regimen with Will and we've been listening to Neutral Milk Hotel for the past three days. I have graduated high school and just turned nineteen.

That was Heidegger Stairwell's first tour.

Heidegger Stairwell finished recording with producer Sly Dog Mac in May, two years after Lugh lost his eye, Torq found Coco, and three months after losing the Battle of the Bands. Coco came home to Emmet Lake for the summer and Torq quit his construction job so he could focus on the band full-time. The rest of us graduated high school that June, with Isis Wong the last in our class to walk. I almost didn't walk out of protest.

For three months the band had been calling me Evan. I'd been dressing as a guy for a couple of years, and androgynously most of my life. Freshmen all thought I was a guy, until a senior "corrected" them or they saw me coming out of the girl's washroom. Even old Mr. Wakefield, the fossilized head of the math department, accepted that I was male, and often told me to "take that hat off, young man." So for graduation, which meant fuck-all to everyone but me, I arranged to walk in the male gown. It was going to be my official silent coming out. It had to be silent, because I'd been looking for words since the Battle of the Bands and they didn't exist.

But when I received my graduation package, my gown was white. I didn't know if it was political, malicious or just an oversight. But I couldn't bring myself to wear that white gown on stage; I couldn't even put it on, not over the suit Torq and I had put together from his father's closet.

My parents, who drove up for the ceremony, went after the administration. My sweet wren of a mother raged at the vice principal, the principal, and the secretaries and then took over the office phones trying to contact someone at the school board who gave a damn. My father went to Canadian Tire, bought a can of blue spray paint and threatened to paint the gown if someone didn't get me the right colour. It was a circus.

My parents didn't know why they were doing it. I asked my mother recently why she fought so hard for me that day over what could have been construed as a fashion statement. She told me, "Honey, your father and I didn't always know what you needed or how we could help you get through everything that was obviously hurting you. But that time we knew exactly what you wanted from us, so we did it. I wish we could've been more successful. But you had Lugh."

Lugh solved the problem in a way only he could.

"Switch gowns." He offered me his blue gown.

I told him we couldn't do that—he needed to wear a blue gown too. I said this as he was taking the white gown out of the wrapper and donning it. It was only a little short; I'm tall enough myself and he only has a couple inches on me.

"Lugh, take that off," said my father. "We'll get this sorted."

"It's fine. It fits." Lugh fastened the snaps.

"Honey, this is a girl's robe. We need to get you both blue ones," said my mother, reaching for the snap at the front.

As respectfully as he could, Lugh shrugged her off, grabbed the blue stole, and slipped it around his neck. "Problem solved. See you in there, Ev." He walked off down the hall. A couple of our classmates saw him and laughed, asking if he was a girl now. To which he replied: "I'm just me, man."

He wore a blue and white eyepatch for the ceremony. And I wore my blue gown.

If anyone noticed my coming-out statement, they didn't say anything. Coco, who watched from the audience, told me blue was my colour. Everyone else just commented on how "pretty" Lugh looked in his virginal white gown. It made him blush, so they just teased him more.

The next week we went on tour.

Heidegger used some of the Mooseknuckle money to buy a used cube van. It wasn't as sexy as some of the band buses they've used since, but after we spray painted it, furnished it with a fold-out couch and daybed bolted to the floor, a futon stacked against the wall, and two beer fridges running through the lighter receptacles, it became a home away from home. Torq, as expected, was in charge. Coco stressed him out while he was driving, so she either rode in the back of the van or with Will, who'd inherited his parents' Grand Caravan after graduation. Isis rode with Torq. Pierre rode with Will so he could look at the horizon line and not throw up. And so that he wasn't in the same car as Torq. Lugh and I usually rode in the back of the cube van so he could spend the time practicing and I could laze around and tell him how sweet his guitar playing was.

Heidegger's schedule started them on the north shore of Lake Huron and ended in Saskatoon. Twenty-two shows in thirty days at small town bars all along the Trans-Canada highway.

Our first stop was the town claiming to have had Canada's first "Woman Mayor." Heidegger played at a little pub filled with middle-aged jean jackets and dirt-smudged campers who probably hated listening to us almost as much as we hated them. The second was a little town mostly there to service the adjoining reservation. People there listened respectfully enough until a couple of guys got drunk and "Freeman Shuffle" ended up the soundtrack to a barroom brawl. Somehow Torq and Will ended up in the middle of it. When I saw them jump in, I poured all the CD money I'd collected in my pocket and punched an old guy in the stomach. He was the bar owner's uncle and I got thrown out.

We ended up in the town closest to Emmet, at a community centre instead of a bar. Heidegger Stairwell played to a half-full hall populated with straight-laced teens and fluffy white-haired arts enthusiasts. After the concert, many of them bought CDs for their grandchildren and half of them asked if they could get me a sandwich. One tween girl lingered at the table while I sold the albums, and asked if I wanted to take her to the movies. It wouldn't be the last time a thirteen-year-old girl asked me out either.

Heidegger played two bars in Sault Ste. Marie and sold some CDs. And then we made our way up the coast of Gitche Gumee. There are beaches along that lake that look like postcards from Australia. I couldn't believe our country could look like that, and so close to home. I never gave it enough credit.

We stopped at one of the beaches for a meal and so Torq could rest and Lugh and I could experience sunlight. It wasn't long before Will and Torq stripped off and ran stark into Lake Superior.

"Apparently you can see the site of the wreck of the *Edmund Fitzgerald* around here," said Isis, spreading an old blanket (Will's)

That was Shane Meawasige and Lucky Tremblay. Every time Lugh and I went to visit our grandfather as kids, they came by to chase us off the reserve. Once, when I was working on the highway, I went in to the corner store to buy the foreman some smokes. Those guys saw me pull out my status card and they reported me to a goddamn OPP officer. They told him there was a white guy inside using a forged card. The OPP took me into the station and I almost lost my job. Those idiots had it coming. —**TORQ** on the beach. On cue, Lugh went from playing Buddy Holly to Gordon Lightfoot's song about the ship. I took photos of the girls singing, the sun glittering in their hair, highlighting their bare shoulders, the swell of Coco's cleavage, and the line of Isis's collarbone. Pierre sat in the sand a few metres away. I snapped a photo of him, his neck craned to watch the girls. The second shot I took was of him glaring at me. Isis shucked off her skirt and top and joined Torq and Will in the water.

I sat, rubbed shoulders with Coco. "Gonna go in?"

She said, "I'm having my period."

Coco was lying, but talking about menstruation disgusted me so much that I let it drop. I asked her if she was happy to be back in the North.

She said, "Do you think Torq loves me?"

Pierre got up and walked down the beach. I said, "He wouldn't put up with you if he didn't."

I thought she'd roll her eyes, tell me what a jerk I was, but she didn't. "I used to think you were in love with him."

Lugh stopped playing.

I snorted. "That's stupid. He's like my brother. He is my brother." I said to Lugh, "Play us some beach music, why don't you?"

Lugh stood. "I need new strings." He wandered back to the van, his long-sleeved grey shirt stained dark with sweat at the pits and small of his back. He wore, and wears, winter clothes all year round.

Coco and I weren't especially close, but I'd known her longer than any other band member. She was also incredibly honest and impartial, except when it came to her ego. So I said to her: "Coco, do you ever feel weird in your body?"

She said, "It's so hot today and I'm all sweaty. You must be boiling. I have an extra tank top. You want?"

"No thanks. I mean, do you ever feel like your body doesn't belong to you?"

She said, "When I eat Chinese food I get really bloated, my hands swell up and I can't wear any of my rings. I'm not fat. My mom said so."

See? "Yeah, you look great." Actually, she'd looked exhausted since Sault Ste. Marie. I had hoped she would return the compliment so I could try to segue into my confession.

"I have cramps," she said. "I've had them for days. That's why I've been moody."

That gave me a chance to confess something else. "Will and I are taking these pills. They make us kind of moody."

"Pills? For what?" She wasn't concerned, just confused.

"They're, kinda like, steroids."

"I get why Will would take steroids—he's getting so flabby. But why would you take them?"

Because I'm a man. I'm a man and from the moment I had the cognitive and linguistic faculties required for self-awareness, I knew there was something wrong with my body. Coco, living in a body that isn't yours isn't like magically being changed into a shaggy dog, or your mother, and having an epiphany that will change your relationship for the better. It's like waking up to find yourself in clothing you didn't put on: pant legs that trip you up, a turtleneck that chokes you, sleeves that restrict the use of your hands, material that absorbs cold in the winter and heat in the summer, shoes the wrong size that make your toes bleed. And everyone says you chose those pieces yourself, shoved your own arms in the sleeves, and that you look perfect. You even have to wear it to bed because it's perfect for that too, even though it makes it impossible to sleep on the side you best sleep on. It covers your whole body so you can't feel the sheets on your skin. You can't reach your sex organ for the scratchy, hard folds of prickly material that won't lie flat. But no one sees it. And when you tell them, they think you're insane because what you're wearing looks perfect to them. That is why I am taking steroids, Coco. And wearing men's clothes. And asking you to call me Evan.

"Because I want to be able to run faster."

Coco thought about that. "It's probably a good skill for you to have since you piss people off and have chicken arms. Why did you punch that old man? God, why did Torq punch that Native guy? He's always going on about his Native brothers and then he beats one up unprovoked. So impulsive. Drives me crazy."

The devil joined us on the beach, shaking his hair at us like a dog. Coco yelled at him, which was exactly what he wanted. Torq inserted himself between us, dripping everywhere. He wrapped his arms around Coco, ended her trademark shrewish harangue with a sloppy kiss.

> Fact: This is misogynistic. —**ISIS**

> And just plain sexist. —**ISIS**

Coco shoved Torq away. "Can you go find Pierre? I don't know where he went," she said, pulling the blanket out from under him and shaking it in the wind. She got sand in all our eyes.

"Coco, he's a grown man," said Torq. "He's fine."

"We have to leave soon so we can find somewhere to sleep since you didn't book us a hotel room like I told you to. I'm tired of sleeping in the van and peeing at Tim Horton's."

Torq groaned. "What is wrong with you? You've been such a bitch lately."

I mouthed, "She's on the rag."

He said, "No she's not. That was last week."

She growled. "Shut up! I'm tired of everyone knowing every minute detail of my life." She left, yelling, "Find Pierre, Torq."

Torq put his clothes on over his wet skivvies. "And I was hoping we'd get to leave him here." He looked around. "Where's my brother?"

"He went for new strings."

Torq said, "He just changed the strings."

I'd forgotten about that.

"What's he pissy about, then?" Torq frowned. "I tell you, touring sucks."

"That's what happens when you're a rockstar," I said.

"We're not there yet, Ev." He wandered down the beach, whistling and calling out "Pierre, here boy."

An hour later, everyone found, everything packed, we hit the road, the snaking coastal route turbulent, especially in the back of the cube van. The cymbals shivered in their box and at every bump I was afraid the futon was going to fly off the bolt and launch me into the instrument pile. Lugh was quiet, the guitar in the open case. Those strings didn't look new. I asked him what was wrong. He didn't answer me. He was so stoned; he'd hotboxed the cargo cab. It didn't take long for me to start buzzing. I put Neutral Milk on the CD player and melted into the futon mattress, dispersed into the atmosphere, became an electron and went on a sound adventure, frolicking with a billion other particles circling the sun in a land of music clouds, soft and sweet. I drifted from cluster to cluster until I found my atom, my band particle. I was the seventh electron. The particle looked like nitrogen, which was very upsetting because I never thought I would have to think about science again. Then I saw Lugh and we merged into a two-headed boy and we walked the sound paths slowly, to a cacophony of trumpets and ever-present strumming.

I didn't feel the tire blow, didn't hear Torq and Isis yelling, didn't feel the truck heave and stop, precariously perched on a cliff overlooking the sea. I remember the sound world becoming very bright and then the communist's daughter stood in the seaweed water and she spoke in the language of trumpets. And she slapped me across the face and left. That was when I saw Lugh and I were no longer the same person. I felt amputated. For some reason his pants were around his ankles. I followed Isis outside. I walked into the guardrail, the only thing separating me from a fifty-foot drop onto jagged boulders.

"The cliffs of insanity," I said. Lugh stumbled out after me. He was now his own person and was even wearing pants.

> Stoner Translation: Lugh's pants were off because Evie was trying to get into them. Literally. She was on top of Lugh trying to stuff her legs in his pants while he was wearing them. —**ISIS**

"Why were my pants off?" he asked, rubbing his eye, the white of which was beige and red and the iris a flat dull greyish.

"Does your glass eye get sleepy?" I remember asking because the question blew my mind. He said he couldn't feel it and lifted his eyepatch so I could check. Compared to his stoner eye, the glass one suddenly looked real. I asked him if his eyes switched places. He poked himself in the good eye to test if it was glass.

Will's van pulled on to the ledge beside ours. I worried the extra weight would collapse the edge and send us tumbling to our doom. No one would ever find our bodies because Lake Superior, they said, "never gave up her dead." I asked Lugh if he would write a song about us if we died. He asked if "we" included him. I assured him it did.

Coco was yelling at Torq for being a shitty driver and blowing out his tire. Isis had a cell phone and she tried calling CAA, but there was no signal, so she walked farther up the road to the highest point of the cliffs. Pierre stood beside Coco. In my haze, he looked like a hummingbird, like he was vibrating. I asked Lugh if he smelled something weird. He said I smelled weird. I smelled my armpits and they smelled like teenage boy. Cool, I said. Coco ran after Isis, told Pierre to leave her the hell alone, told everyone to leave her the hell alone. Lugh asked me what was going on with Coco. I told him she had cramps but she wasn't on the rag. Periods were hilarious. No gross. No hilarious.

Will told me he measured his bicep and it was half an inch bigger than last week. I took off my shirt and asked him if my muscles looked bigger. He didn't comment on my biceps, just that my nipples were hard. I told Lugh to feel my muscles but he wouldn't even look at me until I put my shirt back on.

The girls came back saying they couldn't get a signal and that Will would have to drive them to the closest town, which was probably Sault Ste. Marie. Or, wait, maybe it was Wawa—that had to be coming up soon. They squabbled over the map. Eventually Will couldn't take it anymore and called them stupid cunts.

Isis hated, and hates, the word cunt. In her mind, it is the most offensive word in all of English, and probably Chinese. She turned tail, got in the cube van, then emerged with Will's snare stand. She calmly walked over to Will's van and beat in the driver-side door with it. I giggled and said it sounded like a steampunk factory. Will flipped out on her. She did the same. I fell over Lugh laughing. Coco hit me with her purse and yelled for Torq, who stumbled out from behind the cube van. She told him to fix Will and Isis, and he told her to chill, that they would fix themselves, see? Coco told Torq he was useless. Torq said he felt useless because they hadn't fucked in three days. Then Coco said they hadn't fucked in three days because she had a flare-up from the herpes he'd given her.

Everything after that happened too fast for me to completely understand in my state. But my observations, combined with things I've heard, suggest the following happens:

> No one had an STD. We were talking about something entirely different. I told Evan that. —**COCO**

1) Coco calls Torq a slut and accuses him of cheating on her. Torq accuses Coco of contracting the STD from someone else because she is the skank even though she says she's only ever slept with him. Torq says, like a jackass, that maybe she got them from Pierre, who probably caught them from his drug dealer who is a black robot named Darlene. Torq is talking faster than anyone else because he and Pierre did a line behind the van.

> Pierre's dealer was a kid named Darrel. He was neither black nor a robot, but he wore a black shirt when he was on the job. Darrel was Evan's dealer too. —**TORQ**

2) Pierre denies Torq's accusation. Torq proves himself right by presenting Pierre's stash. Pierre attacks Torq. Will gets in there and beats the shit out of Pierre and dislocates his bowing arm.

3) Isis pops Pierre's shoulder joint back in and steals Will's van to take Pierre to a clinic. She goes north.

> This I regret. I should've gone south—Sault Ste. Marie is much closer than Wawa. —**ISIS**

4) Will, still on his 'roid rage, stands in the middle of the road as a Greyhound approaches. It stops a little too late and taps him. The driver lets him on the bus so he doesn't sue. Follow that van! When Will finds Isis and Pierre, he steals back the van and leaves them in Marathon or Wawa or some other godforsaken place.

> after I stole back my van I drove home, exsept i was tired so I pulled over in bruce mines and fell asleep. I was asleep for like three days cuz I had a cuncushion. —**WILL**

> We were stuck in Wawa for five days. It is the most depressing place on earth. Especially that goose. All it wants to do is fly away. —**ISIS**

5) Coco and Torq break up and Coco leaves the band. Torq accuses her of never believing in Heidegger Stairwell and Coco says she just never believed in him: that he was lazy, unrealistic, entitled and just looking for an easy way out of Emmet Lake. Coco thumbs her way onto a transport as Torq kneels at her feet begging her to stay. She's crying when she gets on the truck and has to kick him off. She goes south.

6) Torq thumbs the road so he can follow Coco, but Lugh doesn't let him. They brawl, Torq jabbering like a cartoon chipmunk, Lugh like a turtle. The entire time, I watch them, murmuring, "I'm a man. I'm a man. I'm a man," but no one hears me, or I don't say it out loud. Torq punches Lugh in the good eye and

grabs a ride with a delivery van. In his coke-addled confusion he goes north.

7) Lugh and I are left on the side of the Trans-Canada in the middle of nowhere with a broken down band bus and no band. We spend the night there, sleeping it off, waiting for everyone to show up so we can finish the tour. In the harsh light of morning, we realize no one's coming back for us. We flag down a car full of college kids who call CAA for us. We drive back to Emmet, which feels changed the moment we pass by the atomic statue.

> Courier.—**TORQ**

> I stayed with my grandparents in Sault Ste. Marie. I was there for a week. I don't know how I feel about reading this chapter. So much of it was really stupid. But now it's dark, considering what happened in Duluth.—**COCO**

NOTE: Maybe the band can add some details. They'll remember more about this than me.—E

Lugh and I stayed at my house, waiting for everyone to come home. Will got back to Emmet a few days later. He came over the first day to play videogames but none of us said anything and he didn't come back. Isis called me later in the week to see if I'd gotten home. Our conversation was brief. FYI, Pierre's fine too, and Coco, she said, pass it along. I told her I'd tell Will and Lugh. No one had spoken to Torq.

Almost two weeks after the fight, the telephone woke me up in the middle of the night. It only rang twice. I found Lugh in the den, his hand white-knuckled around the portable phone.

"She's fine," Lugh said into the receiver after a long pause. There was a long pause before every response. "Yeah. Yeah. Whatever. Yeah, I'll do it. Don't worry. Bye."

He hung up the phone, cradled it in his hands.

"Was that Torq?" I said. Every time the phone rang we both expected to hear his voice, though it was usually a telemarketer. But not in the middle of the night.

"Yeah," said Lugh.

"Finally," I sat. It felt like the first time I could breathe in weeks. "Where is he? What's he been doing?"

"He's in Duluth, Minnesota."

"Doing what?"

Lugh sighed. "He's in the hospital."

"What the f... Is he okay?"

"He sounds like he's eighty years old," Lugh said. "Does the band have any tour money left? How 'bout the CD sales?"

The band's cash box was under my bed. "We have eight hundred dollars here and almost a thousand in the bank," I told him. "And we... have the van."

He nodded. "I need it all to get Torq home."

Torq flew to Sudbury the next week and was transported back to Emmet Lake General Hospital. Apparently they had to sedate him because he refused to get in the van. The MacQueens, Lugh and I were there when he arrived in the parking lot. He was unconscious, his head helmeted, his neck and chin wrapped in gauze, his arm in a sling, a blanket covering his torso and legs. As they wheeled him into the hospital, Mr. MacQueen had to hold his wife to keep her from collapsing from the shock. I kept flashing back to the night Lugh lost his eye and wondered if Torq would make his own sacrifice.

According to Torq, he had been jumped by some drunks after closing time. He didn't tell us why he was in Minnesota, or how he got there, or why they'd targeted him. Considering that an off-duty EMS worker had spotted him in a ditch on the side of the highway, his jaw and collarbone broken, his windpipe extensively damaged, naked and anonymous, he must have really upset those boys. If that sounds heartless and petty, it's because I'm a poor writer and don't know how to deal with writing about what happened to Torq, or how to write about how he dealt with it.

He spent the entire summer recuperating. The money he'd made over the year, that he'd saved to put himself and Lugh through school if the band didn't pan out, went to paying off his American hospital bills. His parents also had to remortgage their house.

Even when he was cleared to go outside, after his cast came off, the wire out of his jaw, and after the bruises around his neck faded, he didn't. He forbid us to tell anyone what happened to him—not Isis, not Will, especially not Coco. He would send me to the tourist centre to spy on her at her summer job. I'd tell him the crazy honest things she said to tourists: "There is a mining museum if you're interested, but it's mostly just core samples, old maps and taxidermy. You're wearing fake leather so I'm assuming you're an animal lover and may not like that. Why don't you try the hiking trails? The bears are alive on those." He'd ask me how she was wearing her hair, if she was wearing high heels—that meant she felt pretty that day—or if men were chatting her up. I reported her fashion choices and always told him that men— old, young, handsome, not-so—were chatting her up, but that she never noticed. That made him smile. It never lasted. I brought him all my CDs, every genre, every time period, Bessie Smith to Patti Smith to Elliott Smith to The Smiths. But he never listened to any of them, and barely made a sound. Like his voice, Torq MacQueen's silence was deafening.

Near the end of the summer, I took him to the park with me. It was a special place where my mother used to bring us to feed the swans and skip stones. We sat in the grass and watched the sun turn Emmet Lake, the actual lake, orange and scarlet, fuschia, purple, then navy. Somewhere, a loon called.

"Are you leaving?" he said. His voice was recuperating, but it was still gravelly and four tones lower than normal.

"I'm supposed to move to Toronto in a couple of weeks."

"Supposed to?"

"Tell me this is just a hiccup, that the band'll be stronger for it, and I'll stay. In a heartbeat."

His laugh was derisive. "Ev, you're not even in the goddamn band."

That hurt. "Am too."

"You know what I mean. You don't perform. You aren't up on stage stockpiling applause to validate yourself."

I said, "That's not why I stay and you know that."

"You stay for the music." He thought that was funny too, but it was a mean humour. There was an edge to him I didn't understand. "Evan, the band's dead."

I had prepared myself to battle him on this. "It's not. They're waiting for you to lead them, to drag them kicking and screaming into your huddle. They need you."

"That's kind."

"It's not meant to be kind. It's meant to remind you that you have a goddamn duty to keep this band together. Your vision, your heart, your band."

He sighed. "Evan, it's done. The band is done."

"Then we'll start a new one," I said, recognizing the desperation in my voice. "You, me and Lugh. We can do anything you want—rock, blues, grunge, acoustic."

"That's just it. I don't want to do music anymore. So move to the city, go to school, start a new life. Stop using the band to define you—figure out who you are already."

"I know who I am."

He sighed again.

"I'm someone who believes in you so much that I will sacrifice my identity for your music."

Torq said, "And besides that?"

"I'm someone who loves you. You and Lugh and all the rest of them."

"That's just another way to say the same fucking thing, Ev."

"And I'm a man."

I blurted it out, because he pushed me, because I didn't have any other answers. My heart flew up into my larynx and my voice cracked on "man," just to undermine my statement.

His smile was indulgent. "I've known for awhile. Thanks for telling me. But that doesn't change anything. Heidegger Stairwell is done."

I'm not sure what I was expecting from him, but something bigger, as befitted the vastness of his personality and melodramas. It was anticlimactic.

"Are you going to tell my brother?" he asked.

"I plan to."

He told me to drive him home.

◆

Talking to Torq made me more afraid to tell his brother, so I told someone else first.

I thought, of all the people I knew, the one who would be the most understanding would be Isis.

We sat on the bed where we'd kissed two years earlier and I told her, blunt, like she would appreciate. I expected some sympathy, or Isis's version, advice. She greeted my announcement with a grimace.

"Are you kidding me?" She got off the bed, like she couldn't wait to be as far from me as possible. She paced the room and turned on me, eyes hot and dark, "You think you're a man?"

I suddenly felt naked and hid my body behind one of her pillows. "I know I am," I said, quietly.

"Fuck you do!" she snapped. "Goddamn it, Evie. You're not a man. You're just . . . you're not even butch. You're just a fucking trendy andro."

I felt like I'd walked into the middle of a minefield. I didn't even understand the terms she used. "I don't know about any of that. I just know that I'm a man inside. I just wanted to tell you. I'll go." I headed for the door. She cut me off, put herself between me and the exit.

Isis is much smaller than I am; I have four or five inches on her and she has those tiny Chinese bones. But as you've figured out by now, she is terrifying, and keeps kryptonite in her pocket just for me. "Why do you think you're a man?"

My words failed me. "Because I know I am."

"But you like men, right? You love their disgusting cocks and their hairy cheeks and burly arms and the apish way they grunt and lumber around. Isn't that right?"

"I like men, yeah," I gave her that.

"So, you're not only a man, you're a gay man," she scoffed.

I couldn't look at her. "Yes."

"So let me get this 'straight.' You weren't just born with the wrong sex, you're also genetically predestined to be gay?"

I didn't like the way she said that. "I know what I am, Isis, stop being a bitch just because I don't fit your narrow world view."

She laughed. "Of course, you being a gay tranny makes so much more sense than you being a crazy misogynistic straight woman."

"How can a woman be a misogynist?"

"Pretty fucking easily, apparently. You hate women so much you can't even stand to be one."

"Isis, I don't want to goddamn talk about this."

She sneered. "You act like a counsellor to simpletons like Will and egomaniacs like Torq, and you start to think you're a lot smarter than you are. But you're fucking naive and you'll realize that when you leave this little bubble. That's why you won't let the band die, isn't it? You're terrified, and you should be." She opened the door. "Get out. Of town. Go be a fucking person, not just a catalyst for other people's lives."

I walked home.

Lugh was on the swing on my porch. I climbed up beside him and buried my face in his shoulder so he wouldn't see I'd been bawling my eyes out like a little bitch all the way home.

"Isis called," he said, draping his arm over my shoulder. "She said she lost her temper with you."

"I don't wanna talk about it." One more word and the self-control I'd been mustering since the end of the driveway would crumble. I just wanted to spend the rest of my time in Emmet playing house with Lugh.

Two nights before I left I woke up and did my walk of the house. I no longer expected Will in the chair, Torq in my parents' bed, or Isis hiding in the guest bedroom, silent as death, but I was surprised when I found the sofa in the den empty. Lugh had gone to see his brother that evening—I assumed he'd fallen asleep there. He hadn't slept at his house in almost six months.

I had a vivid, lucid dream right after my rounds. Lugh came into my room, stood over my bed and watched me sleep. I watched him watch me. The moonlight bisected his face, the right half blank and serene, the left scribbled with sorrow, shame and fury.

I asked him why he had two faces. He said because I did.

Said Lugh, "Are you Evie or are you Evan?"

I said to Dream Lugh, "Evie is dead. Or maybe she never existed."

Dream Lugh pressed his forehead to the wall and wept for Dead Evie.

In the morning, I found Torq on my porch swing.

"I'm sorry," he said.

"I knew you'd come to your senses."

Torq was upset. "Not about the band. I ... I thought he knew."

Dread rumbled like timpani in my belly. "Who knew what?"

"You said you would tell him."

I remembered my dream which meant it wasn't a dream. "Where is he?"

Torq said, "You should've told him."

I found him in the backyard, sitting on the deck steps where I first met him and his guitar. He was petting one of his dogs. When he looked at me, it felt like a cold metal rod through my chest.

"Lugh..."

"I don't understand," he said.

"Let me explain, then." I begged, my voice a desperate octave too high.

He shook his head, stood. "No. I just need some time." He called the dog to him and disappeared inside. I heard the thud of the deadbolt.

I banged on the door, yelling, then screaming, then whispering. I tried the front door and it was locked too. My head didn't fit through the doggy door, but I yelled at him through it. I promised him I was lying, I was faking. I was Evie. I would always be Evie.

I went hoarse. I drank from the dog bowl on the deck. Torq dragged me home. I watched their house from my window and when Torq and his parents went to bed I ran over and checked the doors. They were locked. Torq caught me before I broke a window. He said he would call the cops on me if I didn't go home.

I slept in their garage in a pile of Lugh's old clothes. They made me smell like Old Spice.

The next day, he was gone.

Thieves in the Heat of Anger
1999-2004

November 2011

I'm standing on the street outside the Canadian Embassy in Prague. My suit's charcoal silk, my shirt sky blue, my tie's Pucci, my shoes are Torq hand-me-downs. I smile at a girl across the street; she returns the gesture. She wouldn't have if she walked by me. Close up she would've seen the blood on my collar, the oil dripping from my pores, the grease keeping my hair standing on end. She would've noticed that I smelled like an ashtray and a trash compactor. And maybe she would've recognized me as the guy who pretended to bomb the concert hall.

The aide, a young black woman, pulls up in a sedan. I get in on the passenger side. She is driving me to the airport. I'm being deported. I know you're not surprised, Reader.

"That was a stupid thing you did," she says. "A waste of city resources."

I shrug. "You could say that about any protest. Two well-respected engineers and an architect I happen to admire all told the city that the structure was unsound, a potential death trap in the event of a fire or bomb, and no one listened. I just helped them get attention for their campaign."

"By reporting a fake bomb scare?" she says.

"I didn't report anything. Relied on the kindness of strangers. I just made sure to act super shady."

"You caused a riot."

"Riot? Psh. A glorified fire drill. I was in Vancouver last summer—now that was a riot."

I get a smile out of her for that. "I'm from Calgary."

I say, "I've got a house there."

She laughs. "I know. I heard about your announcement to run as an independent against the Prime Minister. Do you even know anything about politics?"

"Tons. I watch the Parliamentary Channel all the time. That show's hilarious. I think my favourite character is Pat Martin. No—Justin Trudeau—no, Sidney Crosby."

"Sidney Crosby is a hockey player," she says.

"Tch. Hockey is the third branch of government in Canada. Everyone knows that. And you call yourself a spy."

"I don't think causing a bomb scare is going to bode well for your political campaign."

"Fake bombing Europe is going to damage the career of a gay tranny atheist from Ontario campaigning in Calgary?"

She drops me at Terminal 2. I grab my suitcase from the trunk.

"You're going to Germany." It isn't a question. "I hear Heidegger Stairwell's playing Berlin tonight."

"I'll probably check it out."

"Why don't you tour with them anymore?"

I shrug. "Decided to get me a real job. A real life."

"And this is your life? Pretending to blow up buildings, smuggling drugs and screwing with the Prime Minister?"

I pull out the handle of my suitcase. "No, that shit's just funny." I turn away. "Next time you wiretap me, say hello, eh?"

What is my life? I don't even know any more. Sometimes it just feels like I'm doing all these things because shouting isn't working. After every stunt, I like to imagine the band sitting around at breakfast in some fancy hotel, laughing, talking about me, and bonding over it.

> We talk about it. We're not laughing.—**TORQ**

In 1999, they all left Heidegger Stairwell and moved as far from each other and me as possible.

Coco stayed in Toronto, finished her music degree. She taught

112 KAYT **BURGESS**

at a music school in Richmond Hill. After her degree she was offered a place in the Canadian Opera Company ensemble program but turned it down so she could camouflage her talent with the failure that teaching signifies.

Torq moved to Montreal. He worked as a barista, a drywaller, a nude model and became a neo-beat poet. He played Jesus in a well-received production of *Jesus Christ Superstar* and hung out at a lot of karaoke bars. I understand he went through women like two-dollar shirts.

Will went to Western and fought and partied his way through a kinesiology degree. In his last year he knocked up a French girl. They married a month before their baby was born.

Isis moved to Victoria, graduated from the conservatory out there, and worked as a session musician.

Pierre schooled at the Peabody Conservatory and somehow managed to finish a degree and a Masters in four years. During that time he held four public recitals and composed two symphonies, a violin concerto, an indie film score, and two classical albums. He was either bitten by a radioactive spider or using.

And Lugh. Too heartbroken to go anywhere, he stayed in Northern Ontario. He studied classical guitar and performed with the symphony orchestra, but could bring himself to do very little else. His saving grace was the animal shelter down the road where he volunteered four days a week. But only for a few months. When I showed up on his doorstep New Year's Eve, the woman renting the house told me Lugh had moved out three weeks before and she'd heard he took a job up north. Lugh sent me an email a few times a year that said nothing.

I went to journalism school in Toronto. I was the top of my class.

> Fact: Evie had to repeat the first semester because she was lazy and stoned half the time.—**ISIS**

For some bands, this is the end of their story. Not of the individual stories, but the story of the band as living, breathing entity. But if that were the case here, you wouldn't be reading this book.

I finished my journalism degree while copyediting a small political journal which was really just a vehicle for neo-con propaganda. At university I'd had my chance to start fresh, find a world in which no one had ever known Eva Strocker. But I blew that hanging out with artists, post-revolutionary revolutionists, politicos, David Suzuki fangirls, writers and the queer sundry. They all wanted to be others, so they all had eyes for the incongruous, like gaydar for the weird. And, of course, the gay. A vocal slip-up here, a slightly feminine gesture there, and everyone had cause to formulate hypotheses regarding my gender, my sex, my orientation, my sexual predilections, my history, my nationality (someone thought I was a Ukrainian spy) and combinations of the above. Once I knew I was on their radar, I messed with them, flirting with the girls, wearing a kilt, using the urinal (with a funnel).

I told every person something different: I was a boy, I was a girl, I was a hermaphrodite, I was anatomically incomplete, I was a conjoined twin and my brother's head was stuck between my legs and when I needed to pee he sneezed, I fucked boys, I fucked girls, I fucked others, I fucked everyone, I fucked no one.

They stopped asking.

To counteract my days at the journal, me and some of the hipsters I hung out with created an art zine where I wrote music reviews, skewering mainstream acts and lauding every dirty busker in Toronto. The column, such as it was, inspired me to go out looking for music, but I never found what I was looking for because that band had split up four years ago. I'd go home immediately and listen to "Freeman Shuffle" or "O Brother." I rarely heard from anyone in the band, except for infrequent emails from Lugh and the occasional lunch date with Coco. Coco still talked to Isis on a semi-regular basis, who talked to Pierre and, strangely enough, Will.

In November of 2003, I met up with Coco at a cafe in North York.

I didn't recognize her when she walked in—dressed in a tailored suit, her hair poker straight like a curtain around her head. I noticed her nose before her eyes, and her mouth looked thin. It wasn't age—she was only twenty-four—it was life.

She told me I looked good and I hoped she meant it, because I didn't when I returned the compliment. Coco drank green tea and talked about her singing students, all of whom wanted to sing Christina Aguilera and none of whom practiced. I told her about my job at the journal and she told me I was getting more wicked with age. She relayed information about Isis and Pierre, and I told her that Lugh had moved to Thunder Bay to become a lumberjack. In reality I had no idea what he was doing up there. Coco didn't bring up Torq, although I knew she wanted to.

I found her looking at me strangely and asked her what was wrong. She smiled.

"Your clothes, your hair, your mannerisms. I never noticed how very MacQueen they are."

"They were the closest I had to siblings."

"It's more than that. I think you, like, patterned your maleness after them. Which is funny, because their skinny emo asses are hardly paradigmatic."

Coco has always been intelligent, but never philosophical or particularly profound. But that struck me. Sure, I still wore the MacQueens' hand-me-down clothes, and all my style was inherited from Torq, whom I'd always considered a paradigm of beauty; both masculine and genderless. But I hadn't ever considered that it may've gone deeper than that.

> He's really not that handsome. He has weird teeth and eyebrows. He wears makeup and not just on stage. —**COCO**

"Do you ever think about Torq?" I asked her. Because I did and I wanted to share that with her.

She nodded and flapped her eyelashes. Just the mention brought her to tears.

"You won't talk to him?"

She laughed, sharp and short. "He won't."

That was news to me. Last time I checked he'd cheated on her, given her herpes, and run off to whore his way through Montreal.

Coco, embarrassed, confided. No one had ever had any STD. Coco had been pregnant. She terminated without Torq knowing and had panicked and concocted the herpes story. But she'd forgotten that her foetus's father was a MacQueen. MacQueens adopted confused little transboys as their own and wept for stray dogs who may or may not have been menaces to society. MacQueens loved defensive, socially stunted bitches wholeheartedly, even when said bitches told them they were shallow dilettantes. Coco was usually right, but she'd been so wrong about Torq. She knew it, mourned it, and rightfully so.

We went for a walk, her arm in mine, her head on my shoulder. To other couples on the boardwalk, we looked just like them. The men met my eye, checked out Coco, gave me their approval. They had no clue. My new life was incomplete. I had transformed myself from a confused, pain-filled little girl to a man capable of taking care of Columba Coburn. And I would take care of her; I was going to make it all right. I would resurrect Heidegger Stairwell.

When I ended up at the grimy, bed-bug infested refugee camp I called home, I blasted "Freeman" on the boombox. I opened the windows and cranked "Neverending Fire Drill" loud enough for all of Kensington to hear. People flocked in from the street, and my roommates and I flocked out, dancing like druids to an anthem of fire. The CD was on loop and we listened to it for hours until someone called the cops.

My roommates all asked me to burn them a copy. I told them I was only allowed to burn one and that the rest of them would have to find a copy. And then they were only allowed to burn one copy. Thems were the rules. It was a gamble, but I knew about supply and demand. And so the next day I hid copies like little Easter eggs around campus and watched as my roommates spread the word for me, going off on clueless freshmen who found CDs under benches, gushing about the album they saved from the garbage can. When I left school to go to work, there was a buzz, and I'd created it.

Oh, and I did a bunch of other stuff too. To discover how you too can guerrilla market your rock band to stardom, buy my upcoming book, *How to Manipulate Smug Liberal Subcultures into Doing Your Dirty Work*.

> Fact: This is not a real book.—**ISIS**

Two months later I was walking home through Kensington Market and heard "One-Eyed Lugh." I was thrilled, but not surprised as I wasn't far from the hipster ghetto where I'd introduced Toronto to the song. It was coming from one of the new cafes that had popped up amongst the produce carts and head shops. I stopped in for a coffee. The young goth woman at the counter told me she made amazing cappuccinos and that I should have one. I told her I'd be the judge of that and accepted her offer to make me one. From the way she looked at me, I could see she was interested. Living in the anonymity of the city, I was getting used to girls checking me out. I even liked it. I took the coffee. She wasn't wrong about her skill.

"Whose CD is this?" I asked.

"That's Heidegger Stairwell. There are no CDs. Just burns."

The song ended and a cheeseball voice actor advertised ten percent off full-body waxing. So it was the radio.

"If you want, I can give you the link so you can download it. It's not a full CD—just six songs. But they're crazy awesome. I don't even know how to describe this band, they're just so different, y'know?"

Oh, I knew. "So this band's, like, popular?"

"Sort of. This song is. And 'Freeman.' But the band's totally underground—no one knows anything about them. They don't even have a website out. They're like, ghosts or something."

The weblink led me to a network of fansites dedicated to the conspiracy that was Heidegger Stairwell. I spent the whole night looking through message boards. Most people thought it was a supergroup made up of established musicians, and there were as many names put forth as participants in the discussions. No one could place Torq's voice, but he couldn't be an amateur—he just couldn't. People squabbled over lyric analysis, chord analysis. Hidden among the conspiracy theories was the truth—a few posts from people from Emmet Lake High, talking about how they grew up with Heidegger Stairwell, how Will Sacco owed them money, how Torq MacQueen slept with their girlfriend. But none of the conspiracy theorists believed them, because no one on the internet actually went to school with celebrities. Celebrities! They were calling Heidegger Stairwell celebrities.

Two days later, I came home from the job to find a silver Beemer parked outside my apartment.

But this Beemer certainly didn't belong to anyone I knew, because I didn't know the guy standing on my wobbling stairs ringing my doorbell.

"Can I help you?" I called, jogging up, hands in the pockets of my ancient pea coat.

He turned around. He looked mid-thirties, Italian, with a full head of curly brown hair and some chin scruff. His suit was expensive; it caught the light in a way I'd never seen. I envied that suit and vowed to get one just like it when I became rich. Standing there in Torq's old clothes, I probably looked like a Value Village mannequin.

He descended the stairs. "Are you Evan?"

"Who wants to know?"

The guy handed me his business card. Antonio Bonati. Music Management.

"Evan, are you the man to talk to about Heidegger Stairwell?"

Tony Bonati became my greatest ally after I sent him away, checked out all his references and vetted his background. Heidegger Stairwell had become a hot commodity and I didn't want to betray the mystery by handing over secrets to some random douchebag. More than that, I needed to protect my friends, because I would only ever disturb their new lives if I had a perfect alternative. When he proved to be legit—he had already launched several successful alternative acts—I let him in.

He knew he hit a goldmine when I showed him pictures of the band. As magazine editors can attest, they are a photogenic bunch. Tony picked out Torq right away—he looks how he sounds. I told him the story of Lugh's eyepatch, trying not to choke up while saying his name. He admired the picture of Coco and Isis in my backyard in their bikinis, both blistering white under the red sheen of oncoming sunburn. He loved the candid of Will puking in Pierre's violin case, and the tender shot of Torq and Coco lying together at Pancake Bay, taken only hours before the band split. Tony was completely enchanted with Heidegger before he even met them, and that's all I asked for.

"So, where are they hiding?" he asked finally.

I told him. He thanked me for wasting his time and left.

Tony sent a car for me the next day. I was supposed to work, but it was boring so I didn't. The car took me to the airport, onto the tarmac, up to the management firm's jet. Tony was waiting for me on the plane.

"Sit." He offered me a shot of something. I took it. I was on a jet for the first time in my life; I was up for anything.

"Where're we going?" I was just happy not to be at a computer editing copy that told me I was going to hell.

"MacQueen's in Montreal?"

"Last time I checked."

"Then that's where we're going."

Over the course of the short flight, Tony told me he knew Torq was in Montreal. He wasn't exactly inconspicuous, even in a city as big and bizarre as Montreal. They'd tracked him down to a restaurant in Le Plateau, where he served as maître d' and lived in the flat above.

In his crisp white shirt, black pants and suit jacket, with cropped hair and low-key, aluminum-rimmed glasses, Torquil MacQueen almost looked like a regular college-age young man. Almost. Even without a crazy hairdo, the hipster glasses, the cropped jackets, the gold-laced combat boots, he still looked like himself, and people did double takes when they saw him behind his lectern. "Holy fuck, Ev." He grabbed me by the back of the head and wrapped me in his long arms. "What the hell?"

"Hey Torq," I think I said. I may not have had any words. He was crushing me like Heidegger the dog. He kissed my hairline and lingered before he yanked himself away, every gesture dramatic as ever.

"Evan, wow. This is messed up." I'd actually thrown him for a loop.

"Good to see you too."

"Right? Man, Toronto looks good on you. This guy your boyfriend?" He acknowledged Tony, who blanched.

I got in Torq's face and made him focus. When did he get off? He made a joke. When did he get off work? Four. Tony and I took a table and had a three hour lunch waiting for Torq's shift to end.

Torq's apartment was monastic—just a round wooden table, a red sofa, a statue of Buddha and a small television in the living room. The TV wasn't even plugged in. He offered us water or green tea and we sat down at the table waiting for his kettle to boil. As I began to speak, Torq jumped up, interrupting, and disappeared into his bedroom to change out of his work uniform. He came back in jeans and an undershirt. Then he remembered he had beer and pulled three out from under the sink. He downed one and carried the second back to his seat.

"Torq, Tony's a manager"

"Cool. Like corporate stuff, or ... " said Torq.

"I manage bands," said Tony.

"Oh yeah?" Torq winked at me. "Ev likes music. Guess this one's a keeper, eh?"

Tony coughed. "I'm married. To a woman."

"No shit?" Torq finished the second beer. The kettle whistled. Torq unplugged it and grabbed himself a third beer.

I said, "They're playing Heidegger Stairwell."

"Who?" The reluctant question reverberated in the beer bottle.

"Toronto," said Tony.

Torq shrugged. "Cool."

Tony glared at me. I'd assured him it'd be easy. He didn't know I was a liar.

I said, "No, Torq. Like, everybody in Toronto. 'Freeman Shuffle' got leaked and the radio stations got hold of it, and it's all over the internet ... "

"Cool."

I walked to the kitchen and cornered him. "Hey? Focus. Toronto loves Heidegger Stairwell." I said. He played with my hair, touched my arms, my face with his bottle-cold hands. Still no boundaries.

"You did this didn't you," he accused, smiling. "You always do everything."

"Listen to me." I slapped his cheek lightly. "You made it. Seriously, if you come back to Toronto, you are a rock star. Hundreds of thousands of people have heard your music. They are waiting for you yourself so they can worship at your feet. All you have to do is show up."

He smiled, touched my face again. "You still look like a girl when you're desperate." He looked me over. "And you're still wearing my clothes. You need more stuffing in the crotch. Wait, you didn't buy a dick, did you? If you did you need to upgrade."

"Torq, the band..."

He put his fingers on my lips. "Are you staying over tonight? 'Cause if you're not there's this girl I wanna call. She's got pierced everything."

I told Torq not to call any girls.

Tony Bonati spent the night at a five-star hotel and Torq and I reminisced about the good old days over Indian food and Sonic Youth. After dinner we lay on the floor with the lights off and looked out the window at the man-made stars of Montreal.

"Torq, about the band..."

He put his hands behind his head. "Montreal's got great music, Ev. Better than Toronto."

"No it doesn't," I said. "Because Toronto has Heidegger Stairwell."

He asked me if I had weed. I said I was off it because it made me an apathetic coward like him. He asked me again if I had a dick. I told him no. He chuckled to himself and I asked him what was so funny.

"I just remembered the look on Lugh's face when I told him you were a man."

It felt like he'd plucked that nerve like a guitar string. "It was funny?" I said through grit teeth.

"Fuck no. It was like I just told him our parents died." Despite that, Torq laughed again. "He was a damned fool. Everyone else knew what you were. I don't know what he was thinking."

Quiet and dull, I asked him if he'd heard from his brother. Torq said Lugh was a lumberjack in Thunder Bay. No, he was working on a rig in Grande Prairie. Or fishing in Moosonee. Timber rafting in Vancouver. Working pulp and paper in Corner Brook. Mining gold in Manitouwadge. Torq didn't know where Lugh was either. I was as relieved to hear it as I was disappointed.

He put his head on my shoulder. "You hate me, don't you? For ruining your precious band."

I reminded him it was his band.

No, he said. No no no. "It was my music. But we were your band."

I told him that was semantics. He said I used that word wrong or else I would understand it wasn't at all "semantical."

"They'll come back if you do," I said. "You're the leader."

He closed his eyes, wrapped his arms around my waist. "I'm not fit to lead a beetle to shit, Ev." That's where that lyric came from. "Thanks for staying with me," he murmured, rubbing his face against my neck. "I can't sleep alone." The intimacy was confusing. In a certain slant of light he looked so much like Lugh and the music of his cadences sounded like Lugh practicing his licks.

We were both falling asleep, so I attempted one last ditch effort. "Coco misses you."

A tremor shook his body. Just her name was an earthquake. I knew it would crumble him, but I was nervous about what he'd do in his weakened state. He didn't seem structurally sound.

I pressed on: "I saw her a couple of months ago. She gave up on being an opera singer. She's in Richmond Hill teaching singing to little kids."

"That was stupid," he muttered. "She doesn't even like kids."

"People change."

He asked me how she wore her hair, if she wore high heels and what she said.

"She told me about the abortion."

"What did she say about me?"

"Not much. She cried a little."

"She cried?" There was no glee. He was only concerned. "About me?"

"Come back and talk to her yourself."

He said no and was quiet after that.

We left Montreal without Torq. On the plane, Tony asked me if we should go after Coco instead. I said the band couldn't exist without Torq. Torq was the spirit of Heidegger Stairwell.

A week later Torq showed up at my door with everything he owned in the world. It wasn't hard to fit a twenty-six-inch TV and a futon in—I had an extra room—but his clothes were too much for the closet so they ended up in a pile in the middle of the living room floor. I don't know why he brought the futon since he spent every night curled up at the bottom of my bed.

And so we—Torq, Antonio and I—went about picking up the pieces of Heidegger Stairwell.

We flew out to Vancouver to court Isis. She'd moved on, was living with her girlfriend, making a living through music. I convinced Tony to offer Isis a lucrative session gig in Toronto for a month, which she accepted. It was easier to wear down her resolve while she was living down the street. ← *How very cavalier. Evie ripped apart my life, destroyed my relationship and gave me no choice but the band.—***ISIS**

Will wasn't hard to convince. When Torq and I showed up at his door, he introduced his wife, offered us some beer, and took us into his music room, where his daughter was playing with his drum kit. He was teaching high school gym and coaching wrestling. He hated it. ← *i didn't hate it. it was just way harder than drumming.—***WILL**

We should have been wary that Pierre was so easy. He was doing well but he'd racked up debt with some shady characters and once he heard about the EP's success, his irises must've turned to dollar signs. He had us stop for a suitcase and his instruments and he took the plane back to Toronto with us.

Torq went to Coco on his own. He didn't come home for a week. I almost called the police, expecting they'd find his, her, or both their bodies floating down the Humber River. When he came back it was to get his things. Antonio found a condo downtown and Torq moved there with Coco.

HEIDEGGER STAIRWELL

That only left Lugh. And, true to his nature, I didn't need to fly across the country to find him; he came to me.

The night he showed up on my doorstep it was raining, that cold November rain that doesn't feel at all like the song. I almost didn't recognize the man at the door, in his plaid hobo jacket and bushman's beard, not until I saw the scars below his eyebrow and the slightly mismatched irises.

"Couldn't let us go, could you?" Lugh said, finally.

"You're my band," I said.

Nothing more. He was there. He understood what I was. We were good.

I took him in, removed his coat, filled his belly with a hungry man meal. While he ate, I jogged to the corner store and bought him a toothbrush and razor. All he'd brought with him was his guitar. I didn't know where he'd been and I didn't ask, hoping he'd tell me when he was ready. To this day he hasn't given me a definitive answer.

"Thanks," he said when I returned, soaked.

"I don't want you using my toothbrush. You destroy the bristles."

"No. Thanks for getting us back together. We were waiting."

I said, "You could've done it."

He shook his head. "No I couldn't."

A month later they began recording their first album, *A Dog Named Heidegger*. It only took Tony a day to get them a three-album contract.

Wren Sings from Fat Cat's Paunch
SPRING 2004

Scene: a boardroom. Grasscloth walls, crown moulding, piano-lacquer floor. Gold records hang on the walls. The table is long, almost medieval. The back wall is entirely glass and looks out on the Toronto skyline.

Six people sit around the table. No one speaks.

I am leaning against the wall. The Italian suit is beside me, waiting, watching. Nothing is happening. This channel is boring.

I put a box of doughnuts on the table. Nothing. They are bad Canadians.

Then ... someone takes a doughnut.

"I wouldn't, Will. You've put on more than the freshman fifteen."

"Sorry not everyone can live on fish, Ellen."

Torq laughs. "Will's been dying to make a lesbian joke for like four years."

"I've been dying to make a lesbian joke about your hair for the last four minutes," says Isis to Torq. "Is that what they look like in Montreal?"

He runs a hand through his hair. "Montreal wishes."

Coco says, "It's better than whatever Lugh is wearing on his chin."

Everyone at the table stares at Lugh. He's been back in civilization for a week and still hasn't touched the razor.

Pierre asks him, gently, if he has been homeless. Will laughs and chokes on his doughnut. Torq gives him the Heimlich but Will's able to swallow. He accuses Torq of hugging him.

Coco calls everyone's attention to the new tattoo on Lugh's hand, the one that makes it look like his skin has been torn away and he's actually a cyborg. He hides his hands in his pockets. Isis asks him why he'd get beautiful tattoos if he's too self-conscious to show them.

Lugh says, "Because it's not done."

"The tattoo?"

"My body."

"How many tattoos do you have?" says Isis.

"Some."

Isis: "How many more do you need?"

"Some."

"I got one too." Will turns around and pulls down his pants. There is a tattoo on his moon: PROPERTY OF MRS. ANJELIQUE SACCO.

"My wife said I needed to get a tattoo if I wanted to be a rockstar. She didn't tell me what the tattoo was gonna be."

Isis flinches. "Put it away. I can't believe anyone would sign their name to that."

The boardroom sounds like my childhood, full of the rhythmic banter and affectionate teasing of a group of people so tuned into each other it's as though one mind is constructing their conversation. Everything feels right in the world.

Tony says to me, "Is this them getting along?"

I tell him they've missed each other horribly.

Tony took the band to the lounge. He and I sat on the white mod sofas while the band checked out the instruments Tony had assembled. A twenty-piece kit for Will, complete with hand drums, maracas, a kettle drum and three-toned timpani; a nine-foot Steinway for Isis and a couple of Korg keyboards; a Vuillaume violin for Pierre and a Chow cello; a four-string MM bongo, a Courtois flugelhorn (Coco prefers them to trumpets), a

> Fact: It's spelled Cao. —**ISIS**

Buffet oboe and an antique concert harp; Lugh got an Ibanez Rg7 CST; and Torq was handed a mic.

"You expecting a concert or something?" Torq said.

Tony replied, "Not at all. Just have fun with the instruments. We always have them lying around."

"Still remember how to hit things?" said Torq to Will.

"Still remember how to sound like a cat in heat?" Cymbal crash. Will set up his kit to his perfectly OCD specifications.

"I don't know how to play a harp this big," said Coco.

"Focus on the middle strings." Pierre demonstrated. "Ignore the extremities."

"Pierre, I think your violin needs tuning," said Torq, his voice sharp. "Right Evan?"

I agreed, even though Pierre hadn't played the violin yet.

Tony leaned over and asked, "Is there a problem there?"

I told him it was nothing to worry about.

Lugh jammed by himself in the background, bent over the guitar, his cyborg hand drifting up and down the neck of the seven-string, his human hand wielding the neon-green pick like a tiny rapier, infusing Satriani licks with a lyrical passage of hybrid hammer-on/Carter scratch before transitioning into a Vai-and-Stravinsky inspired sequence. The band all stopped to listen to him. Lugh didn't notice he had an audience. He drifted through various scales, modes and keys, but always returned to the golden key.

D major. Lugh was joyous. His joy filled the room, shaking the windows, bouncing off the cement ceiling. Lugh stopped. He saw me, gave his secret smile.

"You learn that lumberjacking?" I said.

"The term is logging." He played a quick run up the neck. "And I never said I was a logger. Nice guitar," he told Tony.

"Would you get over here?" said Will to Lugh. "This is supposed to be a group tug." Torq checked the levels on the amps and took centre stage. Lugh joined him

Torq asked the group what they wanted to play. They all said the same thing: you pick, Torq.

Except Lugh. Quiet. "Let's play my song."

"I haven't hit those notes in a long time..." Torq paled, touched his throat. "Fine. Let's try it."

"Heart on your sleeve," said Lugh.

"Play yours out, Louie."

Like riding a bike.

They played half the EP. Tony's mind was blown—I saw it as he listened. The notes were the same as the recording, but there was a new maturity to the way they played. Lugh's technique was more experimental, more informed; Isis had been exposed to new textures. Coco was more spontaneous; Pierre, more confident, too confident. Fatherhood had made Will more patient. And Torq still had those notes.

Tony had them sign the contract: three albums with the Canadian arm of a major label. You know who they are, but I won't mention them here because of all that nasty business in 2007. So, I'm just going to call them THE LABEL and say that EVERY MENTION OF THEM IS FICTIONAL AND HYPOTHETICAL EVEN THOUGH IT ALL ACTUALLY HAPPENED NO I'M LYING so I don't have to worry about libel if I become zealous in my spite. Fuckers.

There was a signing bonus of ten thousand smackers for me, since the band had negotiated me into their contract as their seventh member. I had no qualms about taking the money since I'd been fired and was the only one in the band who had actually done any work over the last four years.

After they jammed at True North Management, Lugh showed me the seven-string guitar. "What'd you think?"

I strummed the guitar. "Not bad."

"Right?" He played a Bach bourée. His fingers tripped around her neck and body with such familiarity. "Tony, is it cool if I borrow her?"

Tony nodded. "Sure. Take her home. Romance her a bit."

Lugh smiled. He would like that. "She deserves some romance."

"Eh, she just needs some hard and fast strumming," I said.

"That's what I'd do."

"Yeah, but you're a pervert," said Lugh.

"And you're a prude," I countered, childishly.

He brought the guitar home—to our home. And she came willingly—the tramp. After being separated for four years, all I wanted was to sit around, play videogames, watch bad TV, and silently adore the dirty bushman with the Rice Krispies lost in his beard who was sleeping on my sofa. But Lugh and the Ibanez both spoke guitar, and I wasn't fluent. He spent all his time with her, his hands drifting down her neck, caressing her body, admiring her curves, her silky hum, her ecstatic wail.

Bitch.

Heidegger Stairwell began work on their first full-length album. They re-recorded the six songs from the EP, tweaking the arrangements. Between them, they had segments of another five songs that they developed as a band: a couple of new tunes, mostly scraps from Heidegger Stairwell's past life. The label's marketing department was on overdrive trying to develop the band's image. They picked up on the guerrilla campaign I'd started months earlier. Posters went up all over the city.

> Evan "lost" that guitar three times. Once leaving it in the trunk of a taxi, once forgetting it at the airport, and I'm confident he paid a bum to steal it from Lugh in Chicago. Lugh loved that guitar—I've never seen him run that fast. Or at all.—**TORQ**

LOST DOG

NAME: HEIDEGGER STAIRWELL

REWARD $10,000

RETURN TO OWNER
WWW.HEIDEGGERSTAIRWELL.COM

The day the CD went out the band appeared at MuchMusic. When their date with Rick Campanelli was announced, the entire internet seemed to think it was a hoax. But when the lights went up in the Much studio and Torquil hit that first high note of "One-Eyed Lugh," the place was pandemonium.

That was a life-changing moment for me. Until then, they'd been my band, a secret I hoarded. After the televised performance, they belonged to everyone.

I sat on the bleachers with tween girls and groups of college kids who had camped out on the slim chance the band was going to appear. Heidegger Stairwell played a couple of songs, and Much premiered the video for "Freeman Shuffle." The VJ asked them about their lives, their music, their breakup, the curious phenomenon that made stars of them in their absence. They were themselves, razzing each other, one-upping with embarrassing anecdotes. The tweens asked their questions, like "Did you guys always know you wanted to be musicians," and "What would you have done if you weren't in a band." When I called Rick over, the band groaned, chuckled a bit. Rick introduced me as the band's friend—Will yelled mascot—and handed me the mic.

All I said was, "Torq, how does it feel now that you've made it?"

He seemed to look everywhere but the camera when he said, "It feels pretty darn good, thanks."

I gave Rick back his mic. That wasn't the right answer.

A Dog Named Heidegger went triple platinum.

> Fact: Triple platinum in Canada. Just platinum in the US.—**ISIS**

In from the Cold

The Lost Dog tour kept the band moving for a year and a half, first playing seedy clubs across North America, dodgy ones in Europe and, after the Juno win, arenas and concert halls. Torq finally got the tour bus he'd dreamed of when we were kids, and I got to hitch a ride as the official "Band Wrangler," ready and willing to defuse the tense situations. In those days, the fights always involved Pierre, because even though Torq was the frontman, Pierre was writing the new album.

Ole Pierre didn't see much of Europe; he spent his days in the back of the bus with a portable keyboard and manuscript paper. He was never good with criticism in Canada, and he was no different in foreign lands, arguing with Isis about chord progressions, fighting Will on the mathematics of his drum patterns, belittling Lugh's solos while Lugh made ironic jibes Pierre didn't understand. The only person Pierre listened to was Coco and she usually asked Torq what he thought.

Torq was driving me crazy in those days. He was still a frenetic force onstage, but off stage he was distant, which I took personally. For the first few weeks I tried to get him going—teased him, stole things out of his suitcase, played tricks on him like gluing his glasses to a hotel room nightstand or ordering him a tranny hooker or putting caffeine pills in his herbal tea. Sure, he got mad at me, but he forgave too quickly. Remember, he used to beat the hell out of me for that shit. I mentioned this to Lugh. He said

Torq had mellowed and I had to stop worrying. I also had to stop being a dick.

The tour wrapped up in 2006. That was the year I picked up a music column job at the Toronto *Tribune*.

I got the gig based on a joke article I wrote about Heidegger's first week touring. They performed a few gigs around Toronto before starting the Lost Dog tour, but that didn't prepare them for a whole-hog expedition across the continent. They lacked the endurance and stamina. I had energy though, since all I did was mooch off them, so I thought it would be funny to chronicle those weeks, snapping candids of Will sleeping it off in his bass drum; Coco sitting in a motel bathroom crying, mascara dribbling down her cheeks, because she dropped her birth control pill and lost it down the sink; Pierre losing it on a McDonald's speaker box because they didn't have any Filet-O-Fish sandwiches ready; Torq in a hotel hallway wearing only silver lamé boxer briefs, carrying a bucket of ice, explaining to an elderly couple why he was trying to get into their hotel room; Isis smearing mayonnaise all over her scalp after contracting lice from some motel in Syracuse (she ended up shaving her head but I didn't get a photo because she kicked me out), and Lugh, nose red from a cold, stuffing Q-tips up his nostrils to dig the snot out.

> As I understand it, she had to shave somewhere else too. But the *Tribune* is a family publication.—**TORQ**

I tied the pictures together in an article and gave it to Tony a few months later. He sent it to a friend of his who turned out to be editor-in-chief at the *Tribune*, Mr. Sacks, which isn't the old man's real name but the moniker folk gave him because he delegated every task except the gleeful job of firing bullshit writers.

> Evan is the only one who calls him that.—**TORQ**

But he gave me a spread. It was good publicity for the band, great for the paper, fabulous for everyone, even me . . . after the band forgave me for selling out their private moments. I was a pariah for a week. Unclean! Unclean! I had to hang out with the other untouchables, like Tony's assistant, not the hot blonde but the fat guy who always wore an acid-wash jean jacket, and the hypochondriac roadie who looked like an ostrich and seemed to be made of glass whenever equipment had to be moved. The band took the No Evans sign off the clubhouse when I promised Lugh that I'd never write about them again.

Heh.

Anyway, the article led to the column. Once a month I went to places like Brampton, Waterloo or Oshawa to meet amateur rock outfits who had a good sound. Other weeks I'd review bands, shows, albums. But they were barely reviews since anything technical was edited into oblivion. By the time I wrapped up my column in 2008, the *Tribune* had assigned me thumbs up and thumbs down icons.

But the column paid my rent so Lugh didn't have to float our apartment. Yeah, we were still living in that shitbox. I got curtains in 2006 because fans found out where Lugh lived. Lugh didn't notice; he'd sit in front of the window playing his guitar for hours while people set up fold-down chairs on the front lawn and took in the show.

Sometimes fangirls caught me on camera. Rumours spread on the internet about Lugh and his live-in "boyfriend." I didn't tell him; I just bought the fucking curtains and a hidden security camera in case we got wackos.

But I digress. I suppose that's no shock this far into the book.

After the tour, Heidegger headed into the studio for their sophomore album, *In from the Cold*. It was the fastest album they ever recorded because Pierre controlled every detail. It was meant to be his *Pet Sounds*. He took a page out of the Mars Volta playbook and isolated the band members, forcing each to play like a soloist.

More confident! Pierre yelled at Lugh in that nasal nag. You are star of the show!

Lugh played a single decibel louder.

Pierre yelled at him again.

Lugh swayed, like he was more into the music.

Pierre told Lugh that he was a lazy performer and that if he didn't do better Pierre would bring in a guitarist from Peabody. Lugh's counter argument was smoking up behind the studio and passing out.

Pierre'd be at the studio fifteen hours a day, demanding forty or fifty takes. The recording was beating the piss out of him. By the end he resembled Skeletor. No one else seemed to notice because they all hated him for being a tyrant. I remember talking to Lugh about the old days, and why the new album felt so difficult, and he said, "It's because our last despot always smiled when he said we sucked."

Their last despot was unperturbed. Torq laid his tracks, did what he was told, and went home to hide in his Yorkville condo, like being a rockstar was a nine-to-five job.

After Pierre had all the tracks, he dismissed everyone but Coco. Sometimes, when I was at the condo, I would overhear Coco talking with Pierre on speakerphone. He'd have a shit fit about some track, and Coco would soothe him, saying, "I know it's brilliant. Go take a drive, clear your mind."

And Pierre would ask her to meet him. Please Coco, I need to see you.

She would say, of course ma puce, which she always called him.

And Pierre would show up five minutes later, even though the studio was a good fifteen from the condo.

Later, Lugh and I were at the condo because we found a rat living under the couch. I wanted to murder it, Lugh wanted to save it—but when he tried it bit him and he had to get a rabies shot. So, we did what he always did—we walked away, left the rat the house and hoped it would see the error of its ways.

Coco was out with Pierre. Torq was cooking some vegan shit that made the joint smell like Chinatown farts. In that kitchen, in his white chef's shirt (he has costumes for everything), surrounded by plump tomatoes, baby bok choy, and something that looked like a replica of Barney the Dinosaur's cock, Torq seemed like his old self, singing Pink Floyd into a celery stalk while plying us with sake.

The door slammed. Coco's heels clicked on the foyer floor. When she saw us, she smiled. Torq bent down for a kiss, and she gave him a chaste peck.

"It smells horrible," she said, "I wish you'd stop cooking so much cabbage. People are going to think Koreans live here."

Torq stroked her bare shoulder. Coco wore a pink sundress, her copper hair gathered over one shoulder, her lips fire-engine red—smoking hot. But Torq had a faraway look about him. Coco's look of adoration quickly disintegrated into frustration. She kissed him vigorously enough that Lugh and I gave each other the cue to bolt. Before we could sneak out Coco released Torq and said, "Pierre and I went to the Keg for dinner." She walked away, calling, "Where's the floss?"

Then the yelling started. I was a little drunk so this is what I remember.

They screamed about apples and oranges. Judgmental lettuce. With them in the hallway, there was no escape.

Torq said, deflated, "I just want you to be happy."

And Coco, "Ugh! I'm sleeping with Pierre!"

Things got real quiet. I couldn't even hear sirens from the street below.

"No you're not," said Torq, softly.

"You don't know that," she said. The way she said it, we all knew he was right.

"He's not your type."

She either laughed or sobbed. "My *type*? Really? Because he's passionate, talented, intelligent, educated, ambitious, and he treats me like a queen."

"He's selfish," said Torq. "And fragile, and needy. He's everything you hate in yourself. "

She slapped him. The slap echoed around the condo. They had picked the building for its acoustics.

"You're right. He's not my type, because you are my type. Torq MacQueen is the only goddamn man I've ever wanted to be with. That man who lived his art, who dreamed of taking over the world, who fought for every cause with all the conviction he had, who made me love him with sheer force of will—he is my type, and he ruined me for everyone else on this goddamn planet. Including you, because whoever you are, you're not him.

You're just a pliant, timid bore, medicating everyone with bad food."

"People change, Coco." He sounded hard, hurt. "I grew up. You should too."

"Fine. I will."

Her heels clicked down the hall. Torq asked her what she was doing. She told him to move. Torq apologized.

"You don't even know what you did," said Coco, heels clicking, percussive against the bass rolling of a wheeled suitcase.

Torq begged her to stay, said they would eat meat, that he would make love to her every night . . .

"You didn't listen to a word I said," she spat. "Here it is: there's something wrong with you. And you need to figure it out."

"I will. If you stay."

"Do you know why I've been spending so much time with Pierre?" she said. "Because no one else seems to care about this album! Pierre's not a rockstar and he's not Heidegger Stairwell—you are. I'm trying to be you, but I'm not Heidegger Stairwell either. The fans will know. The album is wrong."

The front door opened. Click. Roll.

"Get your shit together, Torquil MacQueen."

Slam.

I'm not sure I breathed until that door closed. Lugh was still holding his joint.

Torq came in, poured himself sake. "Sorry 'bout that."

Lugh looked at him like he was stupid. "Coco wants you to go after her."

"She's stressed out. She just needs some time."

Lugh's jaw tightened. "Really, I think you need to go after her."

Torq slammed the glass on the stone counter. It cracked. "What do you know about women? You've never been with one."

I was going to remind him that *I* had been with one, and that I had sort-of been one, and that I agreed with Lugh, but Torq chucked the glass in the sink and locked himself in his bedroom.

I looked at Lugh. "We should go home, right?"

I did say that, but it was glib. There was that girl in Montreal that summer. And I bought him one during the Lost Dog tour. —**TORQ**

"Do you think the rat's moved out yet?"

I patted his shoulder. "There are stray cats in the alley by the Italian place."

We took the subway home, sitting across the aisle from a gang of shit-talking high-school punks. When I'd had enough, I threw their backpacks onto the platform. The kids didn't make it back.

"We used to talk like that," said Lugh.

"No we didn't. You averaged one word a day and I thought I was a girl."

"You were a girl," he said.

"No I wasn't." I closed my eyes—the fluorescents made my eyes burn. "Do you think Coco was telling the truth? About the album, I mean. I think she was. The album doesn't make any sense to me."

"We should go to the studio tomorrow," he said. "See if Pierre needs help."

For the MacQueens, that fight was huge. I tried to cheer Lugh up by proselytizing to a middle-aged Indian man. Straight-faced and sincere I told him how only by living like Christ would he become like God and be allowed ten nubile wives. My subway evangelizing always got a laugh.

But halfway through my Joseph Smith spiel, I realized Lugh wasn't laughing. He was chatting with a dark-haired girl in a Nightwish t-shirt. She had big eyes and a chickadee mouth and she wrote her number on his arm. It looked like part of his tattoo.

◆

> "In from the Cold *is an album dense as pea soup." "Self-important nonsense, like Omar Rodriguez-Lopez and Win Butler attempting to write a Sigur Rós album on a cello" "Moments of divine musicianship ... overall lacking in the melodic hooks and sheer ecstasy from* A Dog Named Heidegger *that grabbed listeners by the throat and kissed their breath away." "Imaginative, risky, but, overall, tedious, with moments unlistenable."*

The record label pulled half the advertising budget. The band didn't fight it; neither did Tony.

Tony told us that there was a clause in the contract stipulating that if the band didn't sell a certain number of albums by the end of the first two weeks, then the label could renege on the three-album deal and terminate the relationship. It could prove to be nothing, but...

"Aren't you meant to protect us from this shit?" seethed Isis. "Isn't that why you skim so much off our gross, you goddamn jackal?"

To Tony's credit, he remained calm even in the presence of the fire-breather. Will reminded Isis they had a week to pull in the sales. They all argued, except Lugh who hid in the corner with a guitar, and Pierre, who snuck out.

The bathroom had grey stone floors and wooden stalls. There were puffball flowers in a vase on the counter. Pierre emerged from one of the stalls, sniffing, rubbing his nose. "You are here to gloat?" he sneered.

"About what?" I said, leaning against the wall.

"About my failure."

I was taken aback. "Pierre, you can't think I wanted you to fail."

"I know you don't like me, or my music, and you think your precious Torquil is much more smart than me, that he is more important than me. And the fans agree with you." He punched the countertop. "I said to him to help me! I do not know how to do this on my own. Do you know what he said?"

I told Pierre I didn't.

"He said to me that he believed I could do it. It was the kindest thing he has said to me. Or maybe the cruellest because he knew this would happen."

> I thought he could do it. I really needed him to do it. —**TORQ**

"Pierre, they're just a few bad reviews. And those assholes don't know anything about music. They're just using your art to jack off in front of a crowd. I would know since that's what I do."

He turned his fish eyes on me. His pupils were huge. "So tell me what you think of the album. Be honest, Eva."

Eva. I nearly walked out the door. He'd only said my name to my face a handful of times. I buried that new rage and told him what I thought of his album.

It was beautiful, strange. It rarely fulfilled expectations, which was a double-edged sword in his "classical" music, and deadly in the pop arena, even for a band who got away with defying so many conventions. The album as a whole was emotionally distant, as though everything were happening on the other side of a glass pane. "But that's Torq's fault," I said, finally. "Because that's his job."

Pierre nodded. He kept nodding. His whole body was nodding.

I caught him as his legs gave out and we fell to the floor, him convulsing in my arms like a decked mackerel. It probably lasted less than a minute, but it felt like an hour.

When he was finished he threw up on my shirt. Groggy, disoriented, he started to ask me what happened but then saw the puke. Glare. "Lock the door. Get me water. Now."

My hands shook as I turned the deadbolt. I dumped the puffball flowers out of the vase and filled it with water. Pierre sat up, his back against the stone wall. He drank.

"You cannot tell anyone."

"Pierre, that shit is going to kill you."

"What shit? There is no shit. If you tell anyone about this I will kill you." Make sure Evan is telling the truth about this.—**TORQ**

Fifteen minutes later we returned to the lounge. Pierre gave Coco a puffball flower. It was a hydrangea.—**COCO**

Did this actually happen?—**ISIS**

In from the Cold premiered thirtieth on the Canadian charts due to the strength of the title single. But the CD was quickly bumped off by auto-tuned confection. The label used their escape clause and dropped Heidegger Stairwell.

Pierre had a nervous breakdown. The band postponed their tour, and ended up cancelling half the shows.

Coco moved out of the condo, buying a unit in a repurposed nunnery. She said it was the only place for her to go.

Duluth
MAY 2008

The man sitting beside me on the University-Spadina is about forty years old. His thinning cornsilk hair is lightly salted, his nose hawkish, skin porous, jaw stone-cut under a fair beard. He wears a camel coat over a grey suit and carries a weathered briefcase.

He asks me if I'm Evan Strocker, his voice an unexpected tenor. He rifles through his briefcase and pulls out a copy of the *Tribune*. Flipping to my column, he shows me the picture, says: It's you, isn't it?

Of course it is and he knows it.

Seven Days Earlier

Coco sent me across town to check on Torq; no one had heard from him in weeks. Obviously she couldn't go because Hera never cleaned up vomit after Zeus's benders, especially when they were living on opposite ends of Mount Olympus.

I found him on the condo balcony, wearing clothes from high school, his hairstyle similarly dated. He flinched when I tapped on the sliding glass door.

I yelled, "1999 called: it wants its cargos back."

"I need to change the passcode on the front door," he said, closing the balcony door behind him, shutting the blinds. It was a sunny day.

"You don't look hung over," I said. He didn't look good, though. Tired.

He sat on the sofa. "You know I don't drink anymore."

I shrugged. "I don't know anything. Haven't heard from you in almost a month."

He sighed. "I've been busy."

"Busy with what?" I bounced on the sofa beside him. Kept bouncing just to be a dick.

"Obviously nothing to do with you." I think he was aiming for wry but it came out mean.

I waved my hand in his general direction. "What's with the—"

"Feeling nostalgic."

"I always thought nostalgia liked company," I said. "Like misery. They're related—second cousins or once removed or something."

Another sigh. I played through our last encounter to make sure I hadn't pissed him off. Hockey game on the big screen: no red flags. But he was sure mad about something.

As though he could read my mind, his face softened. "How's my brother?"

I shrugged. "Constant."

"What's he think about the hormones?"

Gawp.

"They look good on you."

No one knew I'd started hormone therapy; it had only been a couple of weeks. I definitely hadn't manned up enough to tell Lugh. I told Torq not to blab.

He looked around. "Who'm I gonna tell?"

I was an asshole. "Sorry I haven't been around."

Torq was an asshole too. "Don't apologize—I haven't invited you."

Present

The man on the subway tells me he reads my column every week. He says he's bought and enjoyed several CDs on my recommendation.

Yeah? I say, What's your favourite?

He tells me it's *A Dog Named Heidegger*. But I already know that.

The man on the subway is curious about why I haven't been writing about Heidegger Stairwell lately. I tell him it's because they're on hiatus. Also, I'm not writing about the band because every other paper in the country is and I'm contrary.

Four Days Earlier
While Lugh took his mandolin lesson Wednesday afternoon, I caught the subway uptown. I'd had this nagging feeling since I left the condo. The concierge gave me Torq's mail because "Mr. MacQueen's" box was overflowing. I asked him when he'd seen Mr. MacQueen last. Flustered, uncomfortable, he said he couldn't remember the last time he'd seen Mr. MacQueen.

Torq was asleep in the bedroom, inhabiting only a fraction of the king-size bed he used to share with Coco, the white duvet tucked tight under his chin. Asleep, without the animation of consciousness, he looked like Lugh. I lingered a minute, then closed the door. He seemed fine. I didn't want to talk to him anyway.

On my way out, I passed by the sunken den. The condo was pristine, smelling of lemon and bleach, except that room. Old coffee cups littered the floor, stray leaves of manuscript paper littered the oriental rug, lay strewn across the lid of the grand piano. I picked up the first page of the score and plunked it out on the piano.

No title, no lyrics: only #8 scrawled at the top. The first four bars reminded me of standing with Torq at the gymnasium door listening to Coco sing Rusalka. It didn't sound like "Song to the Moon"—it sounded like him hearing "Song to the Moon" for the first time. The melody spanned octaves, showed painful restraint and unbridled emotion. Even from the simple transcription, I knew the song was meant to support a massive soundscape.

Among the scraps, there were another six tunes written, all rife with spirit, intensity and honesty. I forgot about the tiny world I'd been trying to create with Lugh and remembered the massive one I swore to conquer with Torq all those years ago.

Greedy, I played through everything—even the pages Torq

had chucked in the garbage. Under the piano I found a black metal box full of stuffed envelopes. I couldn't imagine what could be more precious than the melodies I'd found on the piano, but I opened one of the envelopes to see.

I read the letter. I read another. I vomited. I kept reading.

I jumped at the sound of the door opening and turned. Torq stood in the doorframe, his face bloodless.

"Put those back." He said, grabbed my shirt collar and dragged me up the stairs, the lip of each stair stabbing me in the kidneys. I wriggled out of my shirt and rolled, putting the sofa between us.

Torq didn't come after me. He rumpled my shirt up in a ball and buried his face in it. It was a shirt he'd worn, then Lugh'd worn, that I'd stolen from their garage years ago. I still had one of the letters in my hand.

"Who wrote this? How long has this been going on?"

"I'm sorry," he mumbled into the shirt.

"That you didn't tell me sooner," I said.

"That you found out." He sat on the sofa.

I locked the balcony door, drew the curtains. I knelt at Torq's feet, like Coco used to, back in Emmet Lake, when he was consumed by the ignominies of the world.

"This bastard is sick," I said. "We need to call the police."

"He said if I did..."

"Yeah, I read what he fucking said!"

"That's why we can't call the police," he said.

"That's why we are!"

He knew I was right. A wave of relief washed some of the terror from his face. He'd needed someone to shoulder that responsibility and I was his Atlas.

"Torq, some of the details in the letters... they're intimate. Do you know this guy?"

He held the shirt up. "I remember this. I can't believe you still have it."

I asked him again.

He frowned, nodded. "I met him."

"At a show?"

He shook his head. "He was nice. Intelligent. Cool, y'know. His van was really clean. I left my wallet in the tour bus so he bought me dinner."

"You met him on tour? Why would you get in some stranger's van?"

"Because I was geeked out of my fucking mind."

I couldn't remember the last time he got high. "Where the hell were we?"

Torq smiled at the shirt. "You were sitting with the bus near Pancake Bay."

American Mainland, English coastline, Oceania: it took me a moment to remember where that was in the world. I suddenly understood the last ten years of my life. And the band's. "In Duluth. He tried to kill you."

Torq's Adam's apple bobbed hard in his throat, a throat that had been crushed almost beyond repair. He caught me looking at his neck and his hand instinctively went up to protect it. "Ev, he thought he did."

The police arrived, gathered all the letters and photos Torq had received for evidence. I couldn't believe he'd been carrying that for almost a decade. Tony showed up with Coco, who forgot she and Torq were separated when she saw the police, and Lugh, who tucked himself in the corner, out of the way, with me. Lugh asked me what was going on. I told him Torq was being stalked and consequently so were we. No details; Lugh's debilitating empathy couldn't handle them.

Present

The man on the subway asks me if the band is going to start working on a new album. It's been a long time since the last one, or it feels like a long time.

I tell him he should check out Pierre's albums, or Coco's opera, but he's right; it's been a long time. Hell, when you consider *In from the Cold* is essentially Pierre's side-project and *A Dog Named*

Heidegger was just a padded version of the EP, it's been almost ten years since the band made an album.

And that's his fault.

Two Days Earlier

I couldn't look at our La-Z-Boy, the curry-stained sofa, my shitty Ikea double bed, without wondering if someone else had been in them. Every time I drifted off I dreamed up a pair of hands around my throat and woke out of breath. When Lugh woke me up in the morning, I took a swing at him. For peace of mind, he gave me his Swiss Army knife. But I wanted a gun. Or a samurai sword.

The police kept the story quiet and us cloistered. Lugh acted as though nothing had happened: playing videogames, screwing around on his guitar. He only got testy when the police detail told him he couldn't go to his mandolin lesson. He locked himself in his room for two hours and played all his pieces, berating himself the way a teacher might.

But I needed my hormones—I couldn't skip the injection; not when it was starting to take. The fine hairs above my lip were growing in darker, coarser. So I rescheduled my appointment for first thing in the morning, when I knew the cops, at the end of their shift, were groggy and Lugh was asleep. I'd never heard of people being murdered at eight o'clock in the morning on a beautiful May day, so I chanced it, climbed out the window, hopped the neighbour's fence and grabbed a cab on the next street. I was in the waiting room ten minutes before my phone rang.

"Where are you?" Lugh was pissed.

"I'm at Timmy's. I wanted a coffee." Not a bad alibi on short notice, right?

Wrong. "We were just at the Tim Hortons."

Fucking doughnut-eaters. "I just needed to get out. I'll be home in half an hour."

"We're coming to get you."

"Yeah, well, I'm not telling you where I am!"

"We can track your phone."

I asked the nurse if she could put a rush order on the doctoring, as it was an emergency. She looked at my records, assured me I wasn't turning back into a woman and told me to sit down.

Lugh showed up with bedhead and a camo jacket over the tank and jogging pants he usually slept in. He sat beside me. "You're sick?"

I shook my head.

"Then what're we doing here?"

I wracked my brain for an excuse and came up with nothing but the truth. He'd understand—he understood everything. But the last time I sprung news like this on him he took four years to mull it over.

"I'm here for hormone injections."

"Aren't those for menopause?" His mother had gone through it.

"Not oestrogen. Androgens." I added, "Testosterone."

His eye widened. "Oh. Is ... this your first time?"

"Five weeks."

"That's why you have a moustache. And your voice is husky. I just thought you were getting old."

We got home to a squad of police cars, ambulances, fire trucks and onlookers, our side door and carport blown to shit. EMS wheeled off our mailman, who'd triggered the pipe bomb just to deliver a cable bill. If I hadn't gone out the window that morning, I would've been the amputee. Or dead. Lugh had used the front door in his rush to report me missing. But if he'd gone out into the carport that morning, like he did every morning, to have his coffee and smoke a joint . . .

That's when I knew I was going to kill this man.

Present

The man on the subway says he heard about the mailman. He asks me if he's okay. I say he lost his leg. The man on the subway is good at looking sympathetic.

It's taking every ounce of my self control not to slit his throat.

One Day Earlier

The police couldn't pull anything off their surveillance. I watched them walk the perimeter of the house for clues. Everyone went home empty-handed, except our detail who got a pizza and had to stick around for the graveyard shift.

Hours later, I remembered the fangirl cam in the garden. I hadn't checked it years. I pulled the memory card and loaded it on my computer behind a closed door.

And there he was.

I emailed Torq a screencap, with a simple "Do you know him?" in the subject line. I had to make sure.

When Torq called, it felt as though I hadn't seen him in forever. It had only been a couple of days.

"He used to have dark hair. No beard. And the eyebrows are different. He didn't have glasses," said Torq.

"Tell me it's him," I said, rage knotting my stomach.

"Yeah."

He asked where I got the photo. I told him the police. It made me sick to lie to him.

Coco stole the phone. She told me Torq was writing songs again. She brought the phone into the den and told me to listen. "Wait," I said and barged into Lugh's room with the cell phone on speaker, because he needed to hear That Song.

Isis had already recreated the harmony, found the textures, tweaked the transitions so they dragged you kicking and screaming toward that epic chorus. There were no words—Coco vocalized, singing it as though it were a classical master, with the respect she gave everything she sang. It was Torq's song, made for his voice, but having Coco sing it pushed it into the sublime.

Beside me, Lugh hummed his countermelody, tapped out a beat with his foot. In my head I heard the strings—fuck, I heard the entire orchestra with Pierre at the helm—and Will took over from Lugh's foot, invoking that raw tribalism that came from his unexplained rage.

That was Heidegger Stairwell's first jam session in over six months.

When they were done, Lugh tested out a few chord patterns, finger picking, some licks, and they ran it again over the phone.

The music soothed my bloodlust. I promised myself I would surrender the photo to the police.

In the middle of the night I got up for water. Old habits die hard; I checked on Lugh. He lay in a mess of sheets, tattooed arm around the Ibanez, naked arm behind his head. The moon cast a mottled light across his chest, including patches across both eyes. I thought it was the tree, but there were smudges on the window.

Two dots had been drawn on the window with black marker. Below them, scrawled: No eyed Lugh.

I shared the bed with Lugh, the Ibanez, my Swiss Army knife and the fury that kept me pumped full of adrenalin the entire night.

In the bushes by the window I found luck: a receipt for a hotel.

Present

The man on the subway asks me where I'm going. I tell him I'm going to check out a band in North York for my column. They play Viking metal. He asks what that's like and I tell him it's Wagner with an electric guitar.

The man on the subway asks me if it's safe for me to be out and about. I would've thought you'd have police protection, he says.

I tell him the band's under constant surveillance, but I'm low priority. I'm not famous enough to warrant a stalker.

He holds up the photo of me in the newspaper, tells me I'm famous enough. And that I'm rather striking. He's flirting with me and I'm fucking blushing. I glance at the subway map and consider the best stop for killing. And how to get him to follow me to the nearest alley.

I tell him we should go for a drink sometime. Shit, that's presumptuous. You're probably, you know . . . *straight*, I say, as though it were scandalous.

He tells me I have good instincts and I don't need to worry about that. I bet he's loving the irony. I love the irony in the irony.

He smiles and says sure, let's have a drink. He drapes his arm across the back of my seat. I'm a killer, I tell myself. I'm going to kill this evil man. But my hands shake and my heartbeat is deafening. I'm a killer.

But I'm not. I don't know why I'm here; I don't know why I didn't turn over the photo, the receipts. I don't know why I do half the things I do.

I take out my burner phone, tell the man on the subway that I'm messaging the band to tell them I'll be late. I mention a nice place near St. George station that's good for liquid lunches while I text: Lugh, St. George station. He's here. xoxomofo

There are cops at Torq's condo, five minutes away. They have guns and justice. They will save me from my stupidity.

The man on the subway says he knows a place on Sheppard. Cheap drinks, great atmosphere. We should go there.

As afraid I am of pushing this too far and having him bolt, I'm more afraid of him slitting my throat and throwing me in a North York dumpster. I insist on St. George, tell him I have a tab at the bar.

I check my messages and find five from Lugh: 1. Are you okay? 2. We've left. 3. I hate you. 4. I didn't mean that. 5. Police almost there. We're almost there. As I check my texts I take a photo of the man on the subway, in case he kills me. I get another text. 6. I shouldn't have said I hate you. I will only hate you if you get murdered for being a reckless idiot.

The subway is slowing down.

Let's do Sheppard, says the man on the subway, touching the nape of my neck. It'll be worth it.

They don't like my kind up there, I say, no idea if it's true. I was born a woman.

He pretends to be surprised. But he knew from reading my articles, and from following me to the clinic.

The TTC robot announces the station. Out the window I see mint-green painted brick walls, yellow warning lines and anonymous people milling.

I stand; tell him he isn't obligated to go out with me. But he places one hand on my hip, closes the other around my wrist, tells me it's just another thing we can talk about over drinks. North York loves people like me.

Warning bells go off in my head. There is no bar on Sheppard; I will be dead by Sheppard.

The subway doors breathe open. I jump out, pulling him with me. But he lets go and I stumble onto the platform, surrounded by people bottlenecked into the doorway. Police sirens, militant footsteps. I can't let him escape. I jump back onto the train.

He greets me with open arms, laughing about me changing my mind.

I stab him.

I don't remember pulling out the Swiss Army knife, but I know it is the easiest thing in the world, sliding the blade into his abdomen. People around me scream, stampede. The blood splashes warm and wet onto my hand; it feels like washing dishes.

The man stumbles off the train. Someone on the platform calls for security. A guard tackles me. The man from the subway slumps onto his hands and knees five steps away from me. I say over and over, "That man—he's a killer. He killed my Torq. He killed my band."

Then Lugh is at the bottom of the escalator, his old shirt is almost the same colour as the station walls. No eyepatch, no jacket, he is wearing flipflops which he never wears outside the house. When he walks to me, his shoes sound like suction cups. He yells my names—Evie, Evan, Ev.

True to form, I don't think, just react.

After twenty years together I kiss him, grabbing his face and pulling it to mine. It is no paperbag kiss, but I feel life seep into me. He isn't surprised, he isn't hesitant.

Onlookers are taking photos of everything with their phones, but one tourist, a nature photographer, will find the perfect shot: our lips just parted, our foreheads touching, my thumb brushing his puckered eye socket, his face smeared with the blood from my hands. This photo will go viral in the hour. It'll also go in my wallet.

I'm not thinking of this, though. All I'm thinking is: mmm. Also, there is shampoo residue behind Lugh's ear.

In this famous photo, people will assume we are saying profound things to each other, expressing relief and love. But the post-kiss exchange is:

Me: I'm really hungry for grilled cheese.

Lugh: I don't know if they serve that in prison.

Me: Hi Mom. Thought I should tell you that I've been arrested.

Mom: Honey, do you remember that time I took you and Lugh to the waterpark? You snuck an ice cream cone into the pool area and your ice cream fell in the water and they kicked you out, and even though he had never been to a waterpark before and it was all he'd been talking about for weeks, Lugh kicked himself out of the park and bought you a new cone with his allowance money?

Me: Yeah, I actually remember that one for a change.

Mom: I think I'm going to tell that story when you two get gay married. Do you need me to post bail, honey? I'm so proud of you for stabbing that man. ←

Thanks, Ev.—**TORQ**

Fact: As of this time, the court case is still going on.—**ISIS**

♦

"Duluth *is jaw-dropping . . . a mammoth album. A taut set pitting grandiosity against cheekiness, irony against heartbreaking naïveté." "The mythology of this album elevates it to a social experience." "Finally, the album promised by* A Dog Named Heidegger." "A benchmark in the presence of which all factory-produced contemporary music quivers in terror."

NOTE: I don't know how I want to structure this next section, but here will be where I talk about how I stopped the band from begging the label to take them back. Instead, I told them to produce the album themselves, and became their first investor. Maybe I'll talk about all the cynicism that preceded Duluth, especially in relation to the band cashing in on the controversy. Or maybe I'll just gloat about the gross gobs of money I made investing in independently produced art.—E

Be a Better Man
JULY 2009

It was raining, that dark-sky rain that makes the whole day feel like dusk. I often get headaches on those days. I had one that day, but who's to say it was from the rain since that was the day I got kicked out of the band.

But I'll start the day before. I was at lunch with Torq. We were in New Zealand.

"I think you've made it, Torq," I said, raising a glass.

"Almost there, Ev."

Having dinner with him in a rotating dining room overlooking downtown Auckland with its lush tropical trees, eighties-style highrises, eating melt-in-your-mouth mussels and imbibing copious amounts of good pinot, I felt this rockstar was getting a little spoiled. Although, he wasn't eating the mussels, or drinking the wine, and I think they got his order wrong since he was expecting a rocket and they gave him a plate of lettuce, so I guess I was actually the spoiled one.

Five months we'd been touring the *Duluth* album: North America, South America and then Oceania. New Zealand and Oz boasted die-hard fans, so Heidegger Stairwell toured there before the UK. Being from Canada, the band knows how smug that makes overlooked colonies.

Before leaving for the tour, I retired my article in the *Tribune*. I'd said all I wanted to say about new Canadian talent and the artistic influences that created the modern Canadian sound and

> It was nice of Chad Kroeger to drop that lawsuit against Evan. —**COCO**
>
> Torq paid Nickelback a small fortune to drop that suit. —**ISIS**

said more about Nickelback than I probably should've. So I took a contract with *Spin*, writing a review blog and a feature column once a month. The blog, and the column, were called Band Maker, a reference to a joke I'd cracked in an article I wrote for the *New York Times* about drafting the members of Heidegger Stairwell like a baseball manager, analyzing their stats, assessing their star power, fitting them into the most appropriate positions, or stuffing them into positions I needed to fill. (Coco on electric bass for a third of the songs? Why not? Chick bassists are hot.)

When I told the band, backstage at a show in Montreal, Will got pissed. "That's bullshit. Evan did not create the band. It was like . . . I don't know the word."

"Organic?" offered Isis. "An evolution from a shitty three-piece where only one of you could play. No offence, Torq, you're much better now."

Torq leaned back in his chair, arms behind his head. "All my screaming fans would agree with you."

"Don't be smug," said Coco, "The ones screaming for you are fourteen-year-olds who think they're too edgy for Justin Bieber. But I think the name's appropriate. Evan did create us; he's a creepy little puppetmaster."

"Guys, I'm standing right here," I said.

"He didn't make me," said Will, indignant.

"He made you when he punched you in the face for forcing him to wear the bra," said Lugh.

"Fine, then—when did he make you?"

"I made him twice last night," I said and air humped Will just to shut him up. My saying shit like that had the added bonus of embarrassing Lugh, which we'd all been trying to do for twenty years.

Sitting there with Torq on top of the world on the bottom of the world, I found myself feeling nostalgic.

"We should play a concert in Emmet Lake when we get back," he said.

"Funny, I was thinking the same thing."

"Great minds think alike. We could set up in front of the old supermarket, use the parking lot like they do for the Canada Day party. Haven't been home in awhile. Every time I call my ma she bitches me out about keeping Lugh away for so long. And she won't shut up about grandkids." He quirked his eyebrow. "Guess she'll have to stick to nagging me about Lugh from now on."

It took me a couple of seconds to puzzle out what he was saying. "Are you saying what I think you're fucking saying?"

He chuckled. "Keep it down, eh? This place is classy."

"Are you fucking telling me Coco's pregnant?"

"Ev, the swearing. And that's what I'm saying. But no one else knows, so shut up."

The band was having a baby. Lugh was going to be an uncle; I was going to be an uncle. "I can't believe Lugh didn't tell me."

Torq frowned. "What did I just say? NO ONE else knows. Let's talk about something else."

He told me first; I was touched.

Torq pulled a plastic baggie of pills from his pocket and took three. I eyed the pills. "Do I need to stage an intervention?"

"Piss off. They're supplements."

"Your lifestyle is really high maintenance, Torq."

"Says the man getting needles every other week in order to stay a man." It took him a full glass of water to down all those pills. "How's it going? The hormones, I mean. How long's it been now?"

I had to think about it. "Almost a year."

"You look good. I mean you look like a guy, which means you look worse, but the point is you look a guy. Getting the hang of shaving, I see."

I touched my cheek. A delicate thrill buzzed through me when I was reintroduced to the coarseness of my skin and those tiny prickles. "Lugh helps me. He doesn't like my beard."

Torq shrugged. "You look better without it."

"I look fifteen."

"That's wishful thinking. Maybe eighteen." He looked me over, critically. "You seem happy."

"Almost there, Torq." I finished the wine and shook the empty bottle at the bartender. At the bar, not ten steps from us, sat a familiar figure in green jeans, a short-sleeve baby blue shirt and a lime green bow tie. He wore yellow suede sketchers and his hair looked like it had been styled with spunk. I played back our conversation just to make sure we hadn't said anything disparaging about Pierre.

Torq followed my look. "That French fuck..." He marched over to the bar. I threw some money on the table in case we had to leave in a hurry.

Torq grabbed Pierre and spun him around. The stool squeaked. "What the hell, Clowes? You listening in on our conversation?"

Pierre glared. "You are so loud and crass everyone hears it."

Torq, acutely aware we were the centre of attention, thumped Pierre on the back. He was all smiles when he leaned in and said, "You keep your fucking French mouth shut. Coco doesn't want anyone to know yet."

Pierre said, "I don't blame her. I would be embarrassed as well."

Torq's nostrils flared. He was going to say or do something we'd all regret. Fighting with Pierre made Torq a sexist jackass. And a racist. And sometimes violent. It was dangerous for the band to have them together in public like this.

"Hey, why don't we all head over to the tower? It'll be a great bonding experience," I said, cheerfully, patted Pierre on the shoulder.

Pierre looked disgusted. "What is this we are doing?"

"I'm... uh, I'm touching your shoulder."

"No, where is it we are going?"

Torq smirked. "Skyjumping. Hope you like heights, mon frère."

Someone in the restaurant recognized Torq, so when we got out on the Sky Tower's observation platform, there were paparazzi below, all gathered around the big red and white target we were supposed to land on. Torq went first so they could get their fill and leave us the hell alone.

In his yellow, red and blue jumpsuit, rigging wrapped around his waist and crotch like some sort of anime-themed rope bondage, he didn't much look like a rockstar. They attached the big black jump cord to the rigging and dropped him almost two hundred metres toward the target. And then he was on the ground, getting his picture taken, the wind in his hair, waving to the cameras.

Pierre snorted. "He is a clown."

"Oh man, I love jumping off shit."

Pierre gave me his sidelong glance. "Do you swear because you t'ink it is masculine or because it is how someone raise you?"

A woman in black shorts helped me into the jumpsuit. "My parents are good people," I said. "I swear because I like the percussive nature of four-letter words."

He seemed to accept it. "You have a good ear. It's too bad you're thoughtless and unfocused." Classic Pierre.

I said, "Not everyone has your discipline."

"There are ways to develop discipline even if you are naturally stupid." He glanced down. "They love him because he's handsome. They fawn on him and he loves it more than anything."

"Not more than Coco," I said, steadfast.

"He is bad to her."

I laughed. "He's better to her than she is to him. I love Coco, but she gets off on fighting." ← Take that out. It's libellous. And I very much doubt Pierre said these things.—COCO

"Don't talk about her with your filthy mouth. Of course you take his side."

"What do you want me to say? That's he's an idiot? That he's abusive? That the band could do without him? Come on—you can't be that deluded."

"You talk to me of deluded? You think you are a man."

I pushed my anger deep into my belly. "I don't have to validate myself to you."

"You are just a woman with a beard. And every night a man makes love to you knowing what you truly are." He looked at the skywalk technician. "I will go next."

"I'm already locked in," I said.

"The photographers are here for Heidegger Stairwell," he said.

"Unless you are going to jump without the cable, you are not doing anything stupid enough for them to care about you."

The technician came to rig him up. I said, quietly, "You think you just have to bide your time. But you will never come between them. Especially not now."

His face reddened with fury. "I hate to listen to your voice. It is neither man nor woman—it is grotesque. You are grotesque."

Sometimes the band did that, confront each other passive-aggressively through me. Sure, the words themselves hurt, but Pierre was just parroting. My grotesquerie wasn't *his* preoccupation.

> I would never call Evie grotesque. I hope she knows that. —**ISIS**

Pierre jumped. He was lucky, because I was a whim away from unclipping the cable and pushing him off. Maybe I would've been interesting enough then.

In less than twenty seconds he was down. Torq, in his infinite wisdom, had decided it would be great to let the paparazzi snap Heidegger Stairwell's Lennon and McCartney together. All I saw from the top of the tower was Torq go down with a sock to the nose. Then they were both on the ground, punching, kicking, surrounded by flash sparkles.

> I can't believe Evan is still going on about this. Is he trying to imply Torq and Pierre were fighting over me? We were working on songs for *War Dance* and they were arguing over lyrics. Whatever happened, Evan's completely misinterpreted it. —**COCO**

I looked at the technician. "So, is skyjumping off the table?"

Back at the hotel I found Lugh snoozing, lying on top of the white duvet, as always hugging the Ibanez to his chest. I jumped on the bed beside him and plucked a couple strings.

"How'd it go?" He asked, frog-throated.

"I didn't jump." I jumped on the bed.

"Why not?" He made me sit.

"Because Pierre and Torq ruined everything. By the way, they're in jail for 'breaching the Queen's peace.'"

Lugh gave me a look. "I can't tell if you're joking."

"They beat the shit out of each other on the landing target." I turned the TV on to show him a news clip.

"Guess we're not doing any concert tonight." He turned it off and gave me a tired smile. "Kind of jetlagged anyway."

"Want me to let you sleep?"

He shook his head. "I want you to talk my ear off."

I found myself speechless, for no reason but overwhelming adoration. "You are fucking amazing."

Mysterious smile. "I know, right?"

We lay together, me talking into the evening, the sun fading around us. And when I exhausted everything I was allowed to tell him, I moved on to the one thing I wasn't.

"I need to tell you a secret. It's not my secret, though, so don't go blabbing."

He winked; he hadn't said a word in twenty minutes.

"Coco's pregnant," I whispered. "You're gonna be an uncle."

I wanted him to be excited; to share in my conspiratorial thrill. He was quiet, staring at the ceiling. I asked him if he heard me. He said yes, and it was wonderful. I told him I was going to be an evil uncle, that I'd visit just to hop the kid up on caffeine and sugar. And maybe I'd teach them how to play sports.

Lugh wasn't listening; I'd understandably exhausted his ear. I kissed his pale earlobe in appreciation, nuzzled against the forest of his beard, found his mouth in the thicket. He was tired; I figured he'd be passive, let me molest him and fall asleep before anything happened. But he rolled us over, pinned me with that long ropey body, clutching my hips hard enough I'd wake up with bruises. He pulled away. Breathless, self-conscious, he said, "I want you to let me make love to you the . . . you know . . . normal way."

The Normal Way. He looked ashamed.

"The normal way? What's that? I've never heard of that position."

He looked away. "You know . . ."

"No I don't. What is it?"

"Forget about it." He turned on the lamp, stood up. "I'm tired. I'm going to have a shower."

I jumped off the bed and dammed the opening to the washroom with my body. "Just tell me. How do you know I'll say no until you tell me what it is?"

His knuckles were white at his sides and his lip quivered with anger.

"Say it," I dared him.

He actually looked into my eyes. The right eye was glass, dead, a shade too dark. The left eye held enough life for both of them, enough anger, pain and regret. I hated that both eyes weren't dead.

"Say it."

"I want to make love to you like a man does with a woman. I want to marry you. I want to have children with you."

"You're going to have a hard time with that since the moment we get back to Canada I'm getting the surgery."

Lugh went white. I kept talking, "Hysterectomy, vaginectomy, penectomy, maybe chest reconstruction. In the end, you won't even recognize me."

He turned, went for the door; I went for something closer. I held the Ibanez upside down by the neck. "You fucking walk out that door and I'll smash this."

He flinched, lingered, hand on the door knob.

"Yeah, that stopped you." Fucking guitar. "Lugh, do you see me as a woman?"

"What do you want me to say?"

"I want you to tell me the truth."

Lugh opened the door. I brought the guitar down on the edge of the hotel desk. And again. And a third time.

When I looked up from the cracked neck, fractured fretboard, he was gone. I yelled, "I don't know how you haven't worn away those soles with all the walking away you do." I didn't notice until later that he'd left his shoes.

I stayed up, waiting for him to sneak back in an attempt to bypass our conversation. Every time I heard the elevator, footsteps in the hallway, I turned down the TV and curled up in the dark, waiting. For hours.

Around three a.m. I had a sudden horrible feeling in my gut that woke me from half-sleep. I grabbed my key card, wallet and shoes.

Only one of the hotel's bars was open. I followed the 8-bit sound effects and hyperoxidized air to the 24-hour casino, with its requisite seedy red carpet, Hollywood-licenced slot machines and the elderly tourists pouring money into them. Will was at a blackjack table, sloshed, with a leathering blond bimbo at his side.

I asked him if he saw Lugh. He turned to the girl and asked if her breasts were talking to him. I grabbed his ears and forced him to look at me. The dealer motioned to security, but Will waved them off.

"Have you seen Lugh?"

"Lugh? Sure, he was here like ten minutes..."

Relief. I released him. "Where'd he go?"

"Wait... maybe an hour ago." He looked at the dealer. "How long have I been here?"

"You've been here roughly four hours, sir," said the Kiwi.

Will saluted him. "Okay, so, uh, Lugh was here when I was playing baccarat."

"So more than four hours ago." Panic. Despondency. "Where'd he go?"

Will shrugged. He asked the bimbo to lean over, and he rested his head on her gigantic fake breasts. Eventually he said, "Did you guys have a spat?" He spoke slowly enough I wondered if there was a remote. "He was messed up."

"Angry? Depressed?"

"I don't know. He gave me a hug. MacQueens are such faggots. Well, Torq is. Lugh's just gay. With you." He thought that was the funniest thing he'd ever heard and laughed until his fleshy face turned green and he threw up into the bimbo's cleavage. She jumped back, sending Will tumbling onto the carpet. The pit manager approached with two attendants. They told me he'd won thirty thousand dollars and asked if he would like to cash out. I said to pay him out only in the smallest denominations they had because he liked to count it. Will hates counting. He says he does too much of it as a drummer, but I don't think he counts then either. He hates reading as well so I'm sure he won't read this far in the book. ←

> jokes on you, i just skipped the middle. you gotta take that stuff out about the casino broad. my wifes gonna read this. —**WILL**

I returned to the room. Our room. The bed was mussed, but there were no Lugh-shaped lumps in it.

I went into the bathroom, took all my clothes off, my shoes, my packer, my chest binder. I scrubbed my face, washed off the powder I used to fill in my eyebrows and darken my sideburns. I shaved off my sideburns, the wisps of chest hair, my pit hair, and I shaved my shins. After I moisturized my face, my neck, I pinched my cheeks until they hurt, and rubbed my lips with a washcloth until they were dark and swollen. There was a bottle of bathroom deodorizer and I spritzed it in my hair and under my arms, which stung and would've brought tears to my eyes in the days before testosterone. In my suitcase I had a bottle of lubricant, and I took it to bed with me, got under the covers. I popped the lid, spread my legs open and squirted it inside me, half the bottle, so when Lugh came back in the morning he would find my cunt wet and warm and inviting, all for him.

The bed was too big, so I brought Lugh's broken guitar to it.

I woke up in an empty bed, choking the life out the guitar, my arms scratched and bleeding. Lugh's shoes were in the corner, his banjo lay on the side table, his clothing in a suitcase. My thighs were sticky and the sheets damp. Someone was knocking. I threw on a robe, and opened the door.

Isis stood at the door. Torq hovered behind her, subordinate.

She strode in. "I drove him to the airport," she said. "In the middle of the night. I had to buy him a wallet. And shoes."

I hung my head.

"Are you happy with yourself?" She didn't wait for me to answer. "I knew you were going to fuck him up. I told him you were crazy. He just loved you so goddamn much. And of course you ruined it because of that epic self-loathing."

"That's enough, Isis," said Torq, shutting the door behind him. "Evan obviously feels bad enough—"

"Her name is Evie, Eva Strocker, and frankly, she has spent her entire life hating herself so much that I'm sure this is just a drop in the ocean."

"Do you have something new to say to me, or did you just come to hear yourself speak?" I said.

How condescending that look was. "Goddamnit, you're so selfish. You couldn't just give him one thing. That man pined for years, waiting for you to get your shit together. And you never did, but he still loved you, he sacrificed so much for you, he changed his sexual identity for you because he believes in your delusion. But you need to wake up. You are a straight woman so misogynistic you'd do anything in your power not to be a woman. You're not a man—you just need to be institutionalized."

"Isis!" Torq snapped. "That is not helping."

She laughed at him. "Fuck you and your uber-liberal humanitarian agenda. You want everyone to think you're so open-minded by supporting Evie's psychosis. Your schtick used to be real, but ever since you were fucking quasi-murdered you're like—"

"Isis!" It was my turn to snap. "If you've gotten everything off your chest, then leave."

Her eyes shimmered. "Shit, I didn't want to say it like this. I'm so tired. I just . . . I love you, I love Lugh. I am just terrified that you're hurting yourself, with these hormones and surgeries, and I know you're hurting him. One day you're going to regret all of this, ruining yourself. You used to be so beautiful. I barely recognize you anymore."

"But I recognize myself," I said, my voice surprisingly clear.

"I'm sure you think you do. I'm sorry, I don't believe anything you say." She took a deep breath. "I'm going for a walk. When I get back, Torq, we all need to talk about what we're going to do with this tour. Lugh's gone, Pierre is threatening to leave. We can't do these songs with four people. And you definitely can't do them with three." She left with the last word, wiping her nose with her sleeve.

I envied her tears. It had been over a year since I was able to cry.

"Ev, don't listen to her." He sat beside me on the bed. "She's just being a bitch."

"No she's not," I said. "She's allowed to think what she wants."

"You're not crazy."

I couldn't help but laugh. "I chased your brother out of here last night for wanting to marry me and have children with me. I think I may be."

> I'm not going to ask Evie to change this, because it's accurate. But I wish she wouldn't be so accurate. It sounds so much crueller on the page.—**ISIS**

Forgot to Come for You
MAY 2012

Reader, I could fill another book with what I did in the three years since leaving Heidegger Stairwell, but it would be a waste of time. I've already written about everything I went through, all the musicians I met, artists, politicians, soldiers, scientists, freedom fighters, heroes, villains, saints and assholes. So check out my blog archives, my podcasts, my YouTube channel. Go buy a magazine, or torrent one, I don't care—I was already paid. You better not have illegally downloaded this book though—if you're too cheap, go to the library. If you're too lazy to go to the library, you're probably too lazy to read, so put down this book and get back to picking your nose.

    I left the band and I did things. Like romancing a certain GOP pundit and publically outing myself at her Republican charity lovefest. Then there was the incident in Singapore (deported) and Indonesia (also deported) and Laos (jailed, accused of being CIA, and then deported). Of course, there was the story I wrote about smuggling amphetamines through customs (not in my rectum, by the way, although that doesn't stop the security goons from checking every time), and the ones about the donkey show and riding the running bull. There was that story about rolling a cheese wheel down a hill and crushing conjoined twins in double overalls, but I'm not sure if I made that shit up.

    There was that time I was maced, beaten and mistakenly (I swear) rounded up with Black Bloc scabs at the G20 summit. I was sitting in a detention centre in Alexandria when Mubarak stepped down and, in Forrest Gump style, stood five feet from al-Zaidi when he hurled his shoes at President Bush. And there was my failed documentary about trans-activism in Africa which ended with me stripped, shot in the shoulder and left on hill in Zambia bleeding out. Torq wrote the song "War Dance" about that incident.

> The *War Dance* album cover photo is a still taken from the documentary.—**TORQ**

There was also Prague. I understand Torq is writing a song about that too. As you may have gathered, all Heidegger Stairwell's songs are about me because their lives are so dre-head-fully tedious.

> Egomaniac. Maybe fifteen songs out of the hundreds we've written have been about Evan. It's just that those ones always end up on the albums.—**TORQ**

And, of course, there was the music—incredible music, gamelan-jazz fusion, Nubian folk rock—which led me to these places, and led me to understand them. Frankly, I can't understand shit without a soundtrack telling me how to feel.

No. That's a lie. I choked up at Pierre's wake even without a cello accompaniment.

When Pierre Clowes died he joined the ranks of all the thousand musicians, known and forgotten, who bowed out prematurely, leaving us to speculate on opuses never written. Some of the most beautiful music ever has vanished, entombed between the ears of dead junkies and syphilitics. I suspect Pierre died with music in his head, surrounded by posthumous sympathizers: Purcell, Mozart, Schubert, Bellini, Chopin, Bizet, George Gershwin, Patsy Cline, Karen Carpenter, Keith Moon, Bob Marley, Stevie Ray Vaughan, the 27 Club and all the others.

But in reality, Pierre Clowes died alone of a cocaine-induced heart attack. He was thirty-one years old. At the time of writing, it was five days ago.

The funeral is at the French Catholic church where Pierre and the MacQueens were baptized, where Pierre and Lugh had their first communion. Family and friends, label people and musicians fill the pews. Outside, in the parking lot, on the lawn, lining the chalked-up sidewalks, pilgrims sit wearing skinny green ties,

Heidegger Stairwell shirts or eyepatches, crying, singing or arguing musical theory in Pierre's spirit.

Inside, it's more sombre. Like Pierre.

I get to the church late. I didn't know what to wear. What to be. It took me twenty minutes to decide to shave, a half-hour to pick the violet tie, ten minutes to decide whether I would wear two or three pieces of my suit. I removed and donned my jacket eight times and asked myself if Emmet Lake and Pierre would prefer me with my eyebrows coloured in. I've been feeling strange. Like a balloon loose in the atmosphere that could go anywhere in the universe but back to earth.

I sit at the end of the second pew. Isis is on my right—she saved a seat for me. She wears a grey dress and sunglasses and holds my hand. I haven't seen her since Berlin; neither has the band. My machinations backstage bought them one extra day with her, but they squandered it: Will and Lugh arrested for possession, Torq's altercation with the Berlin Polizei, Coco's public nervous breakdown at the Brandenburg Gate, Pierre's equally public attempt to calm her down by singing the second Brandenburg concerto. But Isis missed them. That was why she went to see Pierre that day. That was why she found him.

Will is beside Isis. His eldest daughter is with him. She's nine. I remember her toddling around practices. She once ripped the hair out of Pierre's bow. To her father's public chagrin and private pleasure, she gave up the drums to play the violin. Pierre used to say she was too good a musician to be Will's child.

My parents sit behind me. I can hear my father breathing. My mother loves all the "kids" in Heidegger Stairwell, but according to the iPod I bought her for her birthday, she listens to Pierre's songs the most.

After the priest speaks and Pierre's sister eulogizes, Coco stands at the altar and sings the Saint-Saëns aria "Mon cœur s'ouvre à ta voix." I've never heard her sing it; it's a piece she's only ever performed for Pierre. Had Torq known that all those years ago, perhaps he wouldn't have dismissed Pierre as a rival so quickly.

Torq sits in front of Isis and me, beside Pierre's mother. He hasn't checked one tear, so he doesn't know he's crying, but he has been since the music started. When Coco's finished, she sits at his side, swiping her thumb across his cheeks. I don't know if they've reconciled, but for the moment they're together.

There's a chair near the lectern. Lugh enters the sanctuary with a classical guitar. No eyepatch, heavy stubble, hair trimmed, tattoos covered. He wears a charcoal suit and a kelly-green tie. Torq will have picked out the suit. Lugh sits, the guitar between his legs, and plays Debussy's "Clair de lune." Pierre introduced Lugh to the piece back when we were kids playing hippie commune at my parents' house on Eden Street. It was the first classical piece Lugh ever played on the guitar.

D flat major. You would think the key to Lugh's melancholy would be B minor, the relative minor to the key to his happiness, but it's not. D flat major is soundtrack to Lugh's crippling, world-shouldering empathy.

But D flat major has always been my favourite key. I've never told anyone that, lest I be accused of blatant romanticism, which would be contrary to my public persona. I suppose I should identify with an everyman key like G, or F, or something unabashedly ridiculous like C flat major. So let's call it C sharp major, then.

Won't change how Lugh feels about it, though.

Lugh disappears into the song. I see the old house, the Young Fogeys sitting in the conservatory: Isis at my mother's piano; Will with a pair of stolen bongos; Coco doing lip trills with a three-string bass hanging off her shoulders; Torq buzzing around the room like a hummingbird; Pierre fiddling with the fine tuners on his violin; Lugh off in his own world playing "Clair de lune"; and me, just there.

Fuck I'm useless. I had one goddamn job to do. Instead I pulled a Lugh.

That day in the bathroom. After *In from the Cold* came out. I should've told someone. I was too petty to care. I should've been the one to find him, not Isis. Torq isn't listening to Lugh, to Coco, to the priest; he's freaking out. Not about Pierre: about the band, the music, the absolute responsibility he's just inherited. Coco won't notice, though: she's thinking about Pierre, the Pierre that existed only in her head, the poor, fragile asexual genius, not the one who was so goddamn obsessed with her he had to prove his worth by transforming into a coke-powered superman.

> Evan has to take this out. All the stuff with Pierre. Coco thinks Evan's blaming her for Pierre dying. It's finally sinking in that Pierre was in love with her and she's losing her mind over it. —**TORQ**

And Lugh can't handle any of it. Once he's finished his piece, he leaves the sanctuary.

Somehow in all of this, William Sacco has come out the mature one, his arm around his daughter's shoulders. I catch him giving her a supportive smile and tremble a little when she curls up against him in the crook of his arm. There's only one person who ever made me feel that safe and I fucking need him right now. I stand.

Isis clings to my hand, her nails dig into my palm. "Where are you going?" she hisses, pulls me back onto the pew.

"I'll be back," I say.

She shakes her head. "I need you."

"I need him."

For a second I think she's going to hit me, or cry, but her lip curls in a sneer. "Of course you do." She releases my hand, stares straight ahead. Her chin trembles. From my vantage point standing, I see Will and his daughter beside Isis, our parents behind, Coco and Torq, Pierre's family, all surrounding her. She's alone.

> Take this out. I don't want Evie using me to emotionally manipulate the reader. —**ISIS**

I touch my forehead to hers, linger, before I say, "I'll come back."

Lugh is sitting on a bench in the Sunday school room, arms around the guitar, improvising on childhood hymns. I'm in no position to be shy, to be coy, to be vengeful, bitter or wounded; I tuck myself in beside him, steal his arm from the guitar, and sink into the connotations of his body, his scent, the accelerating rhythm of his breath. He puts down the instrument and I feel his arms around my back.

"You're missing the funeral," I say.

"There's too much crying," he murmurs.

It takes all my self-control not to start myself. Not for Pierre; for myself, goddamn piece of shit that I am. I feel debilitated by uncontrollable absolution. It has nothing to do with religion—it's Lugh, his nearly boundless grace that I have tested—exploited—over and over again. Like I said, I'm a piece of shit.

"Ev," he says, "we're all worried."

"I'm worried too."

"No. About you."

I know. "Tch. The way you guys obsess about me, you'd think I was the rock star."

Lugh sighs. "You think this is a joke?"

No, but I can't afford to think of it any other way. "Why didn't you wear your eyepatch?"

"Because Pierre hated it."

Of course that's why. Why does Lugh do anything?

He is hesitant when he says, "Ev? What's gonna happen to the band?"

I shrug. "I don't know. It'll never be the same again. Break up, become something else."

"Become what?"

"I guess whatever you want it to be. You can be whatever you want to be."

"Ev, I don't know how to be anything else."

In Berlin, Isis accused me of sacrificing each of the members' identities for the good of the band. Maybe this is what she was talking about. I've always assumed Lugh's dependence on the band, on the music, was his own doing. Considering everything else I've done to him over the years, it's no stretch to think I'm responsible for this too.

Coco and Torq's nanny is at the door. She apologizes, asks if she can use the change table in the Sunday school room. Immediately Lugh distances himself from me, takes the baby, hugs and kisses her and gently lays the giggling two-year old on the Winnie-the-Pooh change pad. He's proficient, effectively wiping and swaddling despite the squirming. When he picks her up, she touches his face, his scarred eye socket, with her doll-like hands.

When the baby and her minder are gone, so is Lugh's smile. And he looks so alone standing in the middle of that room, his arms empty, the tattooed machineheads of the dead Ibanez commemorated on his neck, peeking from under his collar. Alone like Isis. Like Pierre. Like me. I don't want Lugh to die alone. I don't want to die alone. And I'm going to die alone, in a ditch, in fucking god knows where if I keep this up. I don't know what I'm fucking doing. Or why.

All I know is that it's my turn to assume some responsibility for myself. And for Us.

I kiss the side of his mouth, stroking the leaf-vein skin around his beautiful glass eye, which now, aged, has faded to the same colour as the real iris. "I didn't go through with the surgery. I never even scheduled it. I just said that because I wanted to hurt you."

His thick Adam's apple bobs in his throat. "I know. I'm sorry I made you want that."

I rub his back. "I'm sorry about the Ibanez. Actually, fuck that, I'm not. I hated that guitar. She was a smug cunt."

Lugh chuckles in the key of D flat major.

So I say in the key of C sharp major, "You've been everything for me. It's time for me to be anything for you."

His breath hitches in his chest. Modulation to D major. "What does that mean?"

"It means whatever you want it to mean." Perfect cadence in D major.

After the funeral, Heidegger Stairwell, or whoever they are, play "Freeman Shuffle" unplugged. They play for the fans, out on the lawn behind the church, down the hill from the school we all attended, across the lake from where they first performed, in the town where we all were born. ←

> I don't have a good memory like Ev, but the book feels real to me, even if some the details aren't exactly what happened. I support everything he wrote. —**LUGH**

> That's not how the funeral ended. Not for Evan. I forgot my jacket in the coatroom and when I went back I found Evan and Isis in there. Evan was having a panic attack. He was trembling, breathing into his cupped hands. He kept saying "I don't know how to do it. I don't know how to do it for him." Over and over.
>
> Isis told me to leave him alone. But I wanted to help, so I asked him, "What don't you know how to do?"
>
> He said, "Be a fucking woman." —**COCO**

About the Author

Kayt Burgess is a writer, musician and classically trained operatic soprano. She studied publishing at Humber College in Toronto and classical music at the University of Western Ontario, and she earned her Master's degree in creative writing from Bath Spa University in the UK. Kayt was born in Manitouwadge, Ontario, grew up in Elliot Lake and has lived in New Zealand, England and Scotland. She now lives near Toronto.

PHOTO BY
OPHRA ALEXANDRA WATSON

About the International 3-Day Novel Contest

"The deformed left foot of the literary world."—*The Times*

"A coffee-fueled, plot-weaving literary juggernaut."—*Playboy*

"The three-day gauntlet forces instinct to the fore; in the absence of conceptual and rewrite time, the writerly subconscious drives things on."
—*The Globe and Mail*

The 3-Day Novel Contest is a literary tradition that began in a Vancouver pub in 1977, when a handful of restless writers, inspired by legends about Kerouac and Voltaire, challenged each other to write an entire novel over the coming weekend. The dare became a tradition and today, every Labour Day weekend, writers from all over the world try their hand at this intense creative marathon. The contest has now become its own literary genre, one that includes dozens of published novels, thousands of unique first drafts, and countless great ideas.

For more information and for a list of other winning novels published by 3-Day Books and its predecessors, Arsenal Pulp Press and Anvil Press, visit www.3daynovel.com.